GENERATION WASTED

Iriowen Thea Ojo

authorHOUSE®

AuthorHouse™
1663 Liberty Drive
Bloomington, IN 47403
www.authorhouse.com
Phone: 1-800-839-8640

Published by AuthorHouse   10/09/2014

ISBN: 978-1-4969-4510-5 (sc)
ISBN: 978-1-4969-4511-2 (e)

GENERATION WASTED

The American Institute of Child and Adolescent Psychiatric Therapy
New York, NY

Patient:
Jordan V.
16.10 years

Current Assignment:
You will be given a new topic each week.
This is not like an essay for school. Research is not required.
All you need to do is tell your story.

Keira, your eyes are
the streetlights when it's dark out
and I am alone.
-Anonymous

DEDICATION

To my mother, for all the times you lie awake and light your candles for us, and the times you spend wondering where all the years have gone. Yes, your babies are young adults now, but don't let that scare you—we will always be across the hall, buried under the covers, safe and sound in our childhood bedrooms. Never forget how much I love you for all that you've done for my sister and me.

Acknowledgments

For Edugie, because it was an honor to have you practice your monologues with passages from *Generation Wasted*, and to hear you say, "This is actually a book I really want to read!"

For my mom, because you're amazing and you already know why.

For my dad, because you're always the first to smile.

For Mrs. Kane. If not for you, I would have continued believing in limits. You are not just a counselor, you're a motivator. Whenever I leave your office, I feel like I've grown a little bit bigger inside.

For Mrs. Sarich, my AP Literature teacher. Eleventh grade was a super-stressful year, but the great books you taught [and also recommended to] us in class kept me sane, especially since I didn't have any time to spend hours and hours indulging at the library like I usually do. I'm reading *The Fountainhead* now, and loving it.

For Ms. Allie Ireland and Mr. Von Ritche, because without the two of you and all your consideration, both *So You Think You're American* and *Generation Wasted* would be gathering electronic dust in my computer right now.

For Ryan, because you had the patience to read my manuscript and give me the greatest feedback I've ever received in my entire life. Also, you seriously need to publish your own book. I'm serious.

And for all my friends and family who've supported me all along.

Thank you.

April 30, 2012

For Keira's number I had a doorbell ringtone. "Ding-dong," she'd go, when I answered, and I'd say, "Who's there?" And Keira would laugh and say, "Ding-dong, it's me, silly, come open the door," though of course there was no door, just space and her glorious breathing.

It was two-thirty in the morning when she called me, telling me she'd gotten high in a dream and it felt so real and she wanted to take something for it, any kind of shit to make it all go away. It was spring break, slow and boring, except when my phone ding-dong'd after midnight. She was crying so hard that I didn't know what else to do and I was afraid to hang up. I got out of bed, pulled on a shirt and pajama bottoms, and rode my bike to Keira's house.

It was raining and the streets were really dark, yet I could hear cars honking behind me and see red and orange lights flashing in the puddles underneath my wheels. I thought I was slow but I was fast. I mean really.

When I braked, I went flying and scraped both my elbows. I almost couldn't find my phone in the wet grass.

I couldn't ring the doorbell obviously, because her parents were sleeping and it was past three o'clock by then. I thought about doing something romantic like climbing up to her bedroom window, but after some deep thinking I realized there was no way I could get up there, so I called her back and told her to look outside.

Then it was six and I was kneeling beside her bed watching some weird infomercial about blenders, watching her roll and kick and grab at the blankets.

"It's okay, it's okay," I said softly, thinking that maybe my voice could infiltrate her subconscious like music does for people in comas, but then she broke through the surface, sobbing with her hands outstretched, trying to find someone to hold her.

"What is it?"

She buried her face in my neck. I breathed in the smell of her soap. "What was it about?"

She didn't answer at first, but then she started talking about it, and I traced the words into her warm, wet cheek with my thumb: *want, one million, all the time.*

"What are you doing?" she asked me.

I whispered, "Putting your insides out. So the bad dream can leave you alone."

It's something my mom would do when I was a really little kid, she'd hold me in her arms and write my nightmares on my skin like that. Keira took my hand and held it against her chest, and I could feel her beating heart, and she rubbed her eyes and said, "Jordan."

And I said, breathlessly because her heart was under my hand and it felt magical, "What?"

She put her hand over my mouth and then kissed me, and I remember thinking, *God, she's so lovely,* and I said it out loud, and she laughed.

I waited with her until she fell asleep. An hour later, I went back home and got into bed.

It was one of those days; I didn't dream.

ENTRY #1: EXPECTATIONS

Expectations. They'll make or break you.

I used to go to my grandma's house in Martha's Vineyard when I was little, before she got ALS and died, and she was so typical that I could always predict everything she'd do. Like, we'd get up in the morning and run downstairs and she'd be making deviled eggs and cutting bread straight from the fresh loaf and frying sausages. She wore these really thick dresses and skirts that were always really soft, and I remember my brother and sister would go outside to play on the pier and I'd always ask to stay inside with her. I liked sitting in the kitchen. I liked the way the jars of fruit and syrup on the windowsill always had bits of sun in them, and the way she didn't mind the fact that I ate cucumber and lime preserves straight from the jar even though everyone else thought it was gross, and how her soft skirts brushed against my face when I stood beside her at the stove or the counter. Whenever she made me a sandwich she always remembered to toast it lightly. Ajvar was my favorite when I was younger. Ajvar sandwiches or ajvar on bagels. Weird, I know. I hated PB&J.

When she got ALS, she stopped cooking. I stopped sitting at the table in the kitchen and started going out with my brother and sister, discovering the magic that was the pier and the water and all the little shops and all the other grandkids that ran around barefoot in bathing suits and T-shirts. She stayed in her room and read the Bible. I spent the day crabbing and learned that the meat tastes best dipped in lemon and salt rather than soaked in butter. She moved to the hospital.

"Don't worry, I'm fine," she told me. "I'm going to get better soon."

She had to write it down for me to understand her. I thought, *Maybe she's just getting old and shit isn't working in her like it used to.* A stupid eleven-year old. It wasn't really even that I believed her; it was more of me thinking she was going to be okay because she was my grandma, like, I expected her to die in twenty years or something. She wasn't even that old. And I had never known anyone who had died and nobody told me what ALS was. Do you get this? I expected her not to die. But that's what she did, and they told me when I came back from boating with the neighbors' kids, and now I can't eat ajvar without feeling like a total douche.

As for Keira and my expectations of her, I don't even think I wanted that much. What did I expect of Keira? Not to find pills in her sweater pocket. We were on our way to school and she thought I looked cold, so she'd given me one of her hoodies. The whole morning I'd sat at my desk with my hands tucked into the long sleeves feeling sleepy, thinking, *I'm warm, I'm warm*, because of her pink hoodie—like how you feel when you've just had a really nice, long bath and are all fluffy and soft in some old bummy clothing.

Later in the day, after lacrosse practice, I changed back into the clothes and put my hand in the hoodie pocket out of habit, I think. And took my hand out. And was holding a packet of tablets.

They weren't even in a prescription bottle, so I knew something was up. I didn't think it was hard shit because in eighth grade they showed us a bunch of drugs in sealed, adolescent-proof cases. The teachers were like, "This is cannabis, this is methamphetamine, blah blah blah."

Permanent brain damage, collapsed veins, multisystem organ failure, all that. They told us about all of it, and it came rushing back in a flood.

I put the drugs back in Keira's pocket. She was supposed to drive me home so we could hang out at my house before my parents got back, and she met me outside the side doors with this cute, goofy smile, and I got into the car with her and she peeled out of the parking lot. The music was on max, a Florence and the Machine CD, and she'd turned the heat on high and kept trying to talk to me but I didn't want to talk to her.

Finally she said, "What is it, baby? What's the problem?"

I took out the pills and asked, looking through the window, "Are these yours?"

"Shit." She turned off the music. "Where'd you get that?"

"It was in your pocket. Is it yours, Keira? Are you taking these?"

"Shit," she said again. "Fuck. No. It's Farrah's, you know her, right? Farrah Shreve. It's hers, not mine. That's her sweater."

I felt a sudden surge of anger; I'd been betrayed, she hadn't given me her sweater.

"Keira," I said, "are you on uppers?"

Keira stopped the car at the curb, turned off the engine, and looked at me. Into my eyes, piercing piercing piercing.

"No," she said. "No, Jordan, I'm not on uppers."

"You swear?"

"I swear." She tossed the packet out the window, into a tangle of bushes on the side of the road. *Dangerous,* I thought, because what if a little kid found that packet and took it home? *What if she just killed a little kid?*

But we'd already driven away and I was already done holding my breath, because I thought she was telling me the truth and she wasn't using and everything was all right. It was because I expected too much of people back in those days. The old me. People who love you are supposed to tell you the truth, right?

Actually, you know what, fuck this part. I don't even tell the truth.

Entry #2: Popularity

Well, I guess I'm sort of popular. I mean, was. I don't know, really. That's for other people to say, isn't it? Maybe it's because of my brother and sister, who were really popular, or because of Keira, or because I was a theater kid. Not theater as in musical theater—I can only sing in the shower or alone in my room, otherwise I have to hum and even that sounds terrible—but theater as in film.

It's not like I was into acting from the start, though. It was mainly because this Hawaiian transfer student, Kai Kamaka, wanted to be the director of a school play and get it taped and take it to some film festival in the city. In our school the students can't direct anything, which I totally got but he didn't, so he was all, "Let's make our own underground movement, let's make the greatest play ever and enter it in the NYC film festival," and a bunch of people, me included, thought he was a genius. We worshipped him like he was our fucking god. This was

December of sophomore year and I was still dating Keira and she was in rehab so I had nothing else to do anyway.

The first play we did was one of Kai's original masterpieces, "The Rebirth", which was this dystopian story set in the future that was supposed to represent some political movement in the present, similar to George Orwell's inspiration for *1984*. Yeah, he was a political kind of guy, but for once that didn't aggravate the crap out of me.

In "The Rebirth", I played this Jesus-looking character named Asher who really didn't do anything but stand around and hold posters without a shirt on. Kai was apparently against whatever political movement the play was representing, so he tried to make it seem as chaotic as possible. Like the French Revolution, he said. Chaotic.

We filmed it and entered it in a local contest, and it didn't even place. Kai flipped out on all of us, saying we'd messed it up, but in my opinion, we had such lame-ass effects. Actually they were not even lame-ass, they were just nonexistent. Not placing is what happens when you decide to be really freaking cheap.

For this reason, Kai made us pool in money ("Club dues," I told my parents) and said he'd use it to buy some good equipment.

He didn't. He bought a whole bunch of American flags instead, for us to wave in the last scene when everyone was dead. We filmed the whole thing over, reviewed it, edited, brought in props from home, spent hours making props after school in the English wing, and filmed outside in the freezing cold and seven-inch snow. We sent it in to some other contest, a state-wide film festival. By the end of the school year, we found out we'd gotten sixth place and were invited to this really fancy awards ceremony in October. We had to give ourselves a name. Kai chose it, of course, and made us The Depth Crew. We were deep. Or, *he* was.

Everyone at school knew about The Depth Crew by the time we'd submitted the first shitty draft to the festival and Kai became one of the most popular guys in the school, so we became popular too, but really only by association. I guess maybe that's not true popularity. Anyway it's sort of finished now, the Depth Crew, despite the fact that all of us still hang out, because Kai's gone and he was sort of the force behind what we were doing. Maybe I would care if I didn't have too many things to worry about this year. Maybe I'd care if I read more books. I was supposed to take over as director, but after everything that happened, I didn't feel like it anymore so I gave it up to some senior. The senior, this dude who claimed he was destined to win a Tony in the very near future, pretty much destroyed the crew; it's all jazz hands and singing. People complained and I said I didn't care.

"It's not my problem anymore," I said, and that was that. I don't even care.

- 11 -

December 1, 2012

Keira's NA sponsor was this woman named Robin who was addicted to heroin or crack or whatever back in the day, in the nineties.

"You have to accept the presence of a higher power to keep you from using again," she said in a voicemail we listened to in Keira's hospital room. "That's how I got my life back."

"I don't know how I'm going to do it," Keira told me, picking at her red, bitten fingernails. "I can't find any higher power."

"Maybe they mean higher power as in willpower. Or a will to become a better person."

"Well, I have enough of that. I don't need all that higher power stuff. I've got a great willpower."

I wanted to ask her if she was telling the truth. Instead I said, "I guess you have to find some way to accept it. So you can recover."

The recovery part, that was the trigger.

"Jesus *Christ*, Jordan!" she screamed at me. "Why the fuck do you keep talking about recovery like it's an actual process, like it involves you?"

I wanted to say, Please, Keira, don't be angry.

I wanted to say, Please, just do it.

"I want you to recover, Keira."

"It's not about what you want."

"I know. I'm sorry."

She said nothing.

"Keira, I'm sorry."

"Stop," she said. "Stop apologizing. *I'm* sorry, baby. I'm so sorry. I mean, I'm such a goddamn bitch."

She pulled me towards her, held me like I was her kid, kissed the top of my head. Then my forehead. Then my nose. Then my mouth.

"Help me. Help me find this higher power," she said.

And I said okay.

Entry #3: Grief

It's stupid, but what comes to mind is Audra's dog dying. Actually, it was *our* dog, it just lived at her house. We found it on a rainy day, coming back from a study session at the library in Josh's Honda; it was all curled up in a puddle and Audra screamed, "A puppy!" so Nat thought we'd hit it and Josh said we'd get arrested for murder and we all started freaking out.

"Shut up, guys," Audra said, and she got out and picked up the dog and wrapped it in her jacket. The poor animal was shaking and shaking.

Nat said, "Dude, what if it belongs to someone?"

She never took her eyes off of it. "It can't," and anyone could see she'd already become totally attached. Like a mother and her newborn child.

"What do we name it?"

And Audra said, "It doesn't matter," so we decided on Fortinbras because it sounded cool for a dog, even though the dog wasn't really that cool.

So anyway, it was some kind of canine, but I think it must have been part poodle. It was a small dog, black, with curly hair. Every time we went to Audra's house, it would jump on everyone, try to lick our faces, and then try to bite me. I don't know why it was always trying to bite me. That was why I hated it.

One time we were eating these cherry toaster strudel things at the island in Audra's kitchen, and the dog just snuck in out of nowhere and chomped on my ankle. I started bleeding all over the place and Audra's mom had to clean up the blood and get me a Band-Aid and whatever, with stupid Fortinbras *still* trying to get at my torn-up ankle, as if he hadn't eaten anything in twelve years. In record time, the house was filled with my shouting, Audra screaming for me not to kick Fortinbras, and Mrs. Na begging me to stand still. Finally Audra got up off her ass and dragged the dog away so that I could wipe up my leg in peace. Audra's mom, Mrs. Na, started apologizing and spraying disinfectant on my ankle, which hurt like a bitch, and then covered it with about six Band-Aids. I couldn't even shower properly when I got home because of that wound. So it really isn't hard to understand why I hated the dog.

But then it died. What happened was it ran away; it tried to bite me again as Audra was opening the door for me to come in, but the fact that I was wearing boots must've confused the hell out of it and it missed my foot and went hurtling down the road. We drove around putting up lost dog posters and then some weeks later we saw it on the side of the road, a dead body. Audra was so upset that she couldn't even look. She didn't even suggest we bury it or anything, but we did it anyway without her asking. She didn't show up to the funeral. She didn't speak for days. When she finally did, she'd say, "I miss Fortinbras, I miss Fortinbras," over and over, and the rest of us would just go silent. It was sort of easier that way. I felt bad for not caring as much as she did, but I did try my best to make her happy.

pages taken from Keira de Luna's 12th grade journal, date unknown

NA meeting again. Here's a story they say might change my life: there was once a man who married a woman and they moved to a pretty house in a little town in the suburbs of New Hampshire. The man had a small, three-worker construction company, and back in those days (1985 or some shit), he made enough money to afford that nice house with the pool in the yard, which they built a gate around the year after, because their daughter was born in the fall and by summertime they hoped she might start walking.

Their daughter had her grandmother's reddish-brown hair that reminded the woman of autumn leaves, so they named her Willow. She grew up chasing dogs and following her father to work and drawing pictures with her mother at the kitchen table, all things I didn't do because I was too busy memorizing the placements of the seven continents and practicing the fucking violin.

The toddler years passed and the girl became old enough to start school. She made friends and brought them home, had sleepovers at other girls' houses, and went to summer camp. She fell in love with boys. She sat down on her parents' bed one night and said, "Daddy, I have a boyfriend."

Her father nodded and said all right, he wanted to meet him. Her mother agreed, kissed her forehead, and sent her to bed. After that, her father went to the bathroom and cried. My dad didn't cry. He just asked me if the boy got good grades (he didn't. He was in remedial English but I was thirteen and I loved him, at least I thought I did).

The girl's boyfriend's name was Angelo and he was a good guy. He knew how to give a handshake and how to hug a girlfriend. When he broke up with the girl in the ninth grade, her father saw her sob into her pillow and pictured her heart breaking. He wanted to pick her up and swing her around and make her laugh again, because it used to work all the time when she was little. But he was old. And she was growing too fast for him.

These things devastated her. Guys broke up with her. She thought she wasn't pretty enough, she thought she wasn't kind enough, she thought she was too needy. She started believing nobody liked her and that her friends hung out with her only because they felt bad for her. She felt useless and stupid and hideous and alone. Their town was a small one, so she'd see the kids at the store or the mall and their happiness would remind her of how disgusting she was (I don't need kids to show me this, I just need a mirror).

Then she made a friend, who showed her cocaine.

Her roommate caught her using in the dorm and told the dean, who told her parents, who hadn't known. They sent her to rehab. She came back, the same as before.

This girl would go missing for days, but because she was legally an adult, she could go anywhere. They couldn't force her to get help if she didn't want it. They stopped sleeping; how do you sleep if you don't know if she's awake too?

What happened to her was that she died. Twenty-two years old, overdose in a dealer's basement. I saw Jordan close his eyes when tears started streaming down her father's cheeks. The dad was like, "I've told Willow's story a thousand times, but I still…"

I couldn't look at him so I stared at my sneakers instead. I wanted to tell the man he was so brave for coming to this NA meeting to talk about his dead daughter even though it was painful, even though it would always be painful. But his eyes were red and I didn't want to bother him.

In the car, Jordan said, "See, Keira, that's what really happens."

And I was like, "To who," not because I'm that stupid, but because I didn't feel like having this discussion. Especially not with him, because he's got this innocent beauty that allows him to see you as something greater than what you are, with his big adorable doe eyes, as if he's the only one who's figured out that hell is actually paradise.

"To people who use."

"Of course I know that. I knew that even before the presentation."

"It's different when someone says it to you the way he was saying it to all of us."

"Sure, sure, whatever."

He stared at me with what might have been anger, or sorrow, or horror. "Keira, did any of that even register? That girl fucking died! You're not going to *say* anything?"

What did I do? I rubbed my eyes with one hand and said, "I just really want to get high."

Yes, I am a bitch. Jordan started to say something else, and I really wanted him to speak; I really wanted him to say *fuck you*, or *you're such a bitch*, but of course he did not. He just leaned against the window and was quiet the whole way back. Fuck the mirrors. It's him that does it.

ENTRY #4: NEEDS

People are always telling me I need things when I don't. Take my mom, for example. Last year, she, with her motherly-instinct-sixth-sense, noticed that I wasn't "sleeping properly" in the night and thought that I possibly had, like, a brain tumor. My mom is the most paranoid human being in the universe. When we were little, if one of us coughed, she'd think it was something way more serious than it really was. I liked being sick when I was younger because of all the attention I got and not having to go to school and being able to watch TV without my brother or sisters coming to change the channel.

I don't like being sick now because it's such a hassle. After she suggested the brain tumor, she took me to my pediatrician, who checked me out and took pee and blood and then prescribed some meds. It was stupid because I could've taken stuff OTC, which would've been cheaper. But my mom says OTC medicines are often abused. She also thinks space heaters cause cancer. Anyway, she got me sleeping pills and made sure I took them, but they worked so well that I kind of started falling asleep all over the place (while brushing my teeth, taking a French test, playing video games, etc.). I told my mom about it and she took me back to the doctor, who said he thought I should see a child psychologist.

My mom wanted to know why.

The guy said it was for an evaluation.

Just like that.

My mom took me to this shrink in the city. Dr. Scheinberg. She looks like a Wall Street businesswoman, not a psychologist. She gave me a written test that had questions on it like, "On a scale of one to ten, ten being the worst, how alone do you feel on an ordinary day?"

Never, zero, but somehow she concluded that I was depressed and desperately needed intervention before I became absolutely suicidal. I didn't have depression; I just didn't feel like doing anything. But Dr. Scheinberg is my other therapy. See how messed up they all think I am? I mean, I've got two different therapies and I'm really not all that messed up. Maybe just a little bit, but not that much.

Dr. Scheinberg thinks the root of my so-called depression lies in moving to the suburbs and feeling totally isolated, while you guys think it's my unhealthy obsession with Keira that's causing all my problems. No offense, but I don't see how this therapy crap works.

I've been doing it for almost a year now and nothing's changed. I am still me and my parents are still worried and my friends all hate me and my right eye is still fucked up and I keep getting seventies on my English tests, but I'm not supposed to freak out about these things, right? Because they say suffering under schoolwork and all these expectations is not suffering unless we're doing it in an African orphanage, or a hospital room.

They're not going to say, "You need to learn how to breathe again."

They're going to say, "You need a serious reality check."

APRIL 2012

After "The Rebirth", Kai said, "Let's make a play based on *Less Than Zero*."

"What's *Less Than Zero?*" someone asked.

Kai ignored her and held up the book. "This is one of the greatest novels of all time. You guys know *The Great Gatsby*, right? It's like a 1985 version of that, except it's the corruption of the West instead of the East."

We all just looked at him. Some of us hadn't even read *The Great Gatsby* yet.

"Ellis was only 20 when he wrote this," he went on, holding up the book like he was going to throw it at one of us. "Only 20! Can you believe a fucking *kid* made up this masterpiece?"

"I watched *American Psycho* in theaters," somebody said.

"We're not talking about *American Psycho*," said Kai. "You have very irresponsible parents."

Someone else heard there was a movie version with Robert Downey Jr. in it, but Kai said the film was nothing compared to the words and forbade us to see it. He read us his favorite sections.

"The end is the best," he whispered. "Clay—*saw*—the—*light*."

I took the book out from the library and read it and thought it was very good for a 20-year old writer even though the character seemed to have no personality whatsoever.

Kai said, "That's the whole point of the novel. A rich California kid with too much time and money on his hands."

I hated that. That it was a possible reality. It depressed me in the same way that reading all those books about drug addicts did.

For the play, Kai didn't have us audition. He never did auditions; what he did was give you the role he felt your personality was best suited for. I got Julian, Clay's childhood friend. An eighteen-year old hustler and heroin addict.

"What's a hustler?" I asked.

Kai grinned. "Aren't you a city boy, Jory?"

"Well," I said, "yeah, but I mean, not *that* kind of city boy."

He just laughed.

"You know, that's exactly why I chose you for the role," he said.

My initial reaction was, *Shit, I really don't want to portray a teenage hustler/heroin addict.*

But I really wanted to stay in the crew, so I sucked it up and practiced my lines. It felt weird to pretend to shoot up, even if it was fake and there were no needles in the syringes. We performed it at this local university playhouse, and Erin and all my friends came to see it. As Julian, I got a standing ovation. I guess people really liked the fake tears I was somehow able to produce in the scene where I said I was done with the hustling life and the boss dude just plunged the fake syringe into my arm.

Everyone was going to an after party at Kai's house and I was supposed to go, but I said I couldn't. Erin told me she had to go catch the train soon and could drive me back, but I said I didn't want to bother her. It wasn't that I wanted to be antisocial; I *did* want to go to the party. I just had an obligation, that was all.

Keira had asked me to come with her to her first outpatient NA meeting. She'd called me at five in the morning all frantic, saying, "Jor, I've got that meeting thing to go to and, um, I don't think I can do it alone and I don't want to go with my parents and so, um, yeah do you think you can come with me please? Please?"

Half-dead with sleep, irritated, and wiping drool off my face, I said, "Yeah, yeah, I'll come."

I didn't tell her about the play. I didn't want to make her come and get her all pressured about seeing people from school. She'd just gotten out of rehab. It's like rejoining the real world, which hates you.

I kissed my sister goodbye and said bye to the others and got into my car. I was sixteen and didn't have an actual license, just a permit, so I really wasn't supposed to be driving at that time of night, but there were no policemen around as far as I could see. Plus, I didn't look suspicious. But because I can be a paranoid freak sometimes, I avoided any major roads and took a weird route to Keira's house, blasting Nirvana so loud it was hurting my own ears. At the curb, I called her cell and told her I was outside. She came out of the house and knocked on the car window. I rolled it down and turned the music off.

"Hey," she said softly.

"Hey," I said back. "You want to drive?"

Before she could say anything, I got out and went to the other side of the car to get into the passenger's seat. She was behind me, reaching me, bringing me close to her to hug me like an old stuffed toy. She said, "What'd you do today?"

The weather was frigid, but I felt warm suddenly. "Nothing much."

We got back into the car and Keira drove and switched around the CDs in the player.

"God," she said, finally settling on Bloc Party. "Too much punk."

"Whatever." Keira's hands were shaking. "You okay?"

"Yeah, fine, fine."

"No, really." I leaned closer to her, inhaling her scent. The hazelnut shampoo. "Are you nervous?"

"I guess. Yeah. Yeah, I guess so."

"What are you nervous about?"

She shrugged. "Just being there, I guess. It's like, I'm one of *them* now."

"Do you think you are?"

She didn't answer immediately. We were silent for a few minutes, and then she made a turn, and she said, "Well, I *am* an addict."

I didn't know how to respond to that. Keira said, "Jordan, listen."

"Yeah?"

"I'm done, okay? I'm seriously not going back. I am so fucking serious. I promise."

"Keira."

"Because it's not fair to you. Or my mom and dad. Or to my friends. But especially to you. I mean, I don't know why you still stick around."

"Keira—"

"I'm just so fucking sorry, like, for everything I've been putting you through. You don't deserve it. You don't deserve any of it, baby, I'm sorry. I suck, I really do. I'm so sorry, Jor."

I tried to not believe her. I tried to believe her. I rolled the window down again and took deep breaths, because it was all just so overwhelming, I guess, what I thought was authenticity. Keira pulled over, thinking something was wrong, and took me by the shoulders.

"I'm fine," I told her. "I'm okay."

Her eyes went liquid. She held me again and whispered in my ear, "I'm sorry."

My chest ached. Out of relief and sadness. I felt so fucking sad, just then.

"I know," I told her.

"I'm sorry," she answered.

"Don't say that anymore," I said. "I mean, don't say anything."

She nodded against my neck. "Yeah. Yeah."

"I love you."

She nodded again, and sighed.

SESSION: 13   DATE : 12/14/12

Dr. Scheinberg: Jordan, you do know that you were never responsible for Keira, right?

Jordan: Yeah. I guess.

Dr. Scheinberg: You have to understand that you're only responsible for yourself. You're too young to worry so much about other people.

Jordan: But that's not the way it works.

Dr. Scheinberg: ...

Dr. Scheinberg: Then how does it work?

Jordan: I've always had to look after my little sister. My brother and sister have always had to look after me. I was born with things to worry about.

Dr. Scheinberg: [shakes her head] No, Jordan. You're only responsible for yourself.

Jordan: But you *feel* responsible for the people you care about.

Dr. Scheinberg: You mean *you* feel responsible. Not me.

Jordan: Yeah, I mean *I* feel responsible for the people *I* care about.

Dr. Scheinberg: So you're saying you have no choice but to take this upon yourself.

Jordan: Yeah. Because I feel even more responsible when I don't do anything.

Dr. Scheinberg: And how do you feel when you feel…even more responsible?

Jordan: Like crap.

Dr. Scheinberg: Jordan, you can't be Superman. You cannot save the world. You're only human.

Jordan: I know. That's not what I mean.

Dr. Scheinberg: Jordan, do you worry about the people you love?

Jordan: Well, yes.

Dr. Scheinberg: How often do you believe you worry about them? And the responsibility you think you have towards them?

Jordan: Uh, I guess every day? I don't know. As often as it comes to me. Like how anyone would think about the people they love and how they're all doing.

Dr. Scheinberg: …

Dr. Scheinberg: I think you'd do well on anti-psychotics.

Entry #5: Risks

"There are, of course, risks, as with any other surgery."

November, the eye surgery. It's all a blur. All I remember is someone shining light into my eyes, shoving a pamphlet into my hands and saying, "There are, of course, risks."

Of course I remember the minutes before. The surgeon had a mask over his mouth and goggles on with a little flashlight thing attached to them; he was holding the anesthesia mask and trying to get me to laugh at his dumbass jokes. I can't even recall what any of those jokes were, just that they were all dumbass.

"Okay," he said finally, "we're going to put you under. But first, I want you to think of something happy."

"Something happy?"

"Yes. A wonderful memory, a loved one, your school crush…" He smiled at me. He didn't know. "You think you can do it?"

I mumbled that I would try.

When I came to, I couldn't move the right side of my face. Nurses came to change the bandages, and they told me not to cry because of infection or something, so I grunted because I didn't want to scream. My mother would change them after I left the hospital to go back home. She'd talk to me while she did it, as if I were some little kid she was trying to spoon-feed, as if I were four years old and picky. Waves of pain came with waves of nausea, and I'd want to scream but I still grunted instead, even though it wouldn't matter if I shouted in the house; everyone knew that my eye was unfixable, that my left eye was 20/20 while all I saw out of my right were stars and flashes. The doctors said we could try a second surgery in a few months since the first one didn't work out, and as a form of unspoken apology they gave me glasses.

It was not an unspoken apology. The glasses cost an arm and a leg and my parents had to pay out of pocket. One of the lenses was way thicker than the other, but I still couldn't see much out of my right eye, so there wasn't a point in wearing them. The doctor said, "Don't strain your vision. You need to keep wearing the eye patch."

I didn't care about my vision. I wanted to sleep and not think about first surgeries or second surgeries or eye patches and surgeons. Risks, I don't know if I've ever taken them.

Out of Paradise
by Keira de Luna

Harborhill Friends High School Literary Magazine, 2010, pg. 4, "Ninth and Tenth Grade Poetry"

There is this girl who doesn't know how to cry, she waits
to feel anything
When her father tells her, Raise your voice like this
And her mother smiles, thumbs up, *you can do it honey*
When the teachers say, "You have such a wonderful
daughter," and
"I wish she were mine,"
And she goes home so she can hear her father tell her
she should have won first place instead of losing as second
She can't imagine what it would have felt like to be second
When she gets first for that tournament, that competition
this high school
is too big for someone who can never be filled,

except with the echoes of walls that close in with
be better be stronger be like that American or else
"or else"
makes her feel too much.
She doesn't feel.
She just
Feels.

Entry #6: Patience

It's like when I was a kid and my dad would take Francis and me to this place called Orient Point to go fishing. I liked the trip: getting on the road, all of us listening to some book on audio, stopping at the farmer's markets for juice and pie, and going into the store that sold fishing supplies with my dad. Francis would stand with my dad at the counter while he paid and I'd wander around the store, touching things and looking at things until my dad said, "Hey, Jordan, come over here," and I'd go back to them.

I hated the actual fishing, though. We'd stand there for what seemed like hours, without chairs or a bench to sit on. My legs would start itching and Francis and I would just start making shit up—say we'd caught stuff when we knew we hadn't. My dad always said, "Just be patient, boys."

I wanted to impress him, of course, so I stood there and waited for a fish to bite the worm. The worms were sometimes nasty as hell; once I was putting one on a hook and blood squirted everywhere, on my face and in my eyes. My mom wiped me off and my dad told me I'd done it too hard, or something. I was too impatient. That's why I gave up on fishing in the first place. I never caught anything. I always wanted to play in the water instead of watching it.

You could say that, in all seventeen years I've spent on this earth, I have done a lot of waiting. I have been three years old at Whole Foods, holding onto my pants at the checkout counter, crying to my mom who just keeps saying, "You should've peed when we were shopping. If we go to the bathroom now, who will be there to open the door for Erin when she comes home from school?"

I have been nine at Orient Point, calling the fish stupid and ignoring my dad when he tells me to stop shaking the rod, something will bite.

Fifteen, begging Keira to stop. Crying and crying and grabbing her sleeve. It's not even first period yet and we are in the parking lot. She finishes taking the rest of the crushed Vicodin. She tells me not to worry, that she's stopping, that it takes time and I need to stop crying and she's going into a special program.

Then there were doctors who said, "Be patient," that irritability and lack of interest are common in withdrawing addicts. I hold her in my arms when she cries, when she talks about things like having bad dreams and wanting to die. I don't know what to do so I start repeating all the lies the doctors said about being patient and not giving up.

Just like this, you know. Waiting for this therapy to actually start working.

November 2011

It had only been about a week, since Keira had gone to rehab and somehow the entire school knew about Keira and the drugs. I didn't really care that much, except that people kept asking me questions. Then they avoided me. They pitied me. Some of them thought I was a dealer, or I was also on drugs, and rumors spread about why I wasn't in rehab with her.

"It doesn't bother you?" Josh asked me after school one day. "Why don't you just tell people you didn't do anything?"

"I don't know," I'd told him. "I guess I just don't feel like it."

Because I really *didn't* feel like it. And I didn't feel like answering the stupid questions. And I hated having ears, because then I had to hear all the kids talking about how Keira was a spoiled brat who got high just for the thrill. She had to be a brat, because her parents were not divorced, they had money, she got good grades, and she was super popular. Plus she'd already gotten into UPenn early decision. She was a selfish bitch, they said. And poor Jordan Vianney, the naïve little sophomore, he doesn't even know.

My dad said, "You need to break up with that girl."

My mom said, "She's going to get you into drugs, too."

I was like, "I thought you trusted yourselves enough to believe that you raised me well."

"Don't act smart with us!" my dad started yelling. "Why would you want to stay with someone who is a drug addict? Is that the kind of person you want to be associated with?"

"Dad, it has nothing to do with my reputation."

"So then tell me now, Jordan."

"Tell you what?"

"Tell me the truth! Have you been taking drugs?"

"Oh my God. No."

My mom stood up and leaned over me and said, "You don't need to lie us, Jordan."

"No, Mom. I'm not. I swear."

"Then why do you stay with Keira? Is she your dealer? Does she—"

That was when I got up. My dad said, "Sit down."

"No," I told him. "You guys obviously don't know or respect me enough, if you think I'm dating someone just to get drugs."

"Come back here!" my mom shouted, but I ignored her and went up the stairs.

They did this almost every day. They searched my room. They thought I didn't know but I did, because things were always out of place.

I thought that going to see my sister in the city on Saturday would help. I really felt like the whole world was shitting on me—not that I didn't get the reasons why, I mean they were all valid, but I just didn't want *their* reasons. Keira's, I wanted hers. Not theirs.

So the issue was that all my friends were trying to convince me to leave her, and my parents were doing it too, and everyone else was whispering and staring at me like I was some kind of freak. But Erin understands me, and I told myself she'd be different.

She wasn't. I sat across from her at Vine Sushi, stirring the ice cubes in my drink with the straw, staring at my avocado rolls.

"I know you're smart," she said. "I know you make good decisions. Please, Jordan, she'll ruin your life."

I was tired so I didn't say anything.

"You get it?" she said.

I thought about how much I needed to sleep. I thought about how nice it would be to lock my bedroom door and slide under the sheets and sleep forever.

"You get it?" she said again.

Inside of me, Keira was glowing. Her eyelids were falling the way they did when we were alone and she was the girl who tore pages out of dictionaries to hang her favorite words up on her bedroom walls. I imagined her hand, how it used to feel in mine, and it gave me chills.

"Jordan?" she said softly.

I wiped off the condensation around my water glass and asked if I could go home.

ENTRY #7: FREEDOM

When I was in fourth grade, we went on a field trip to Ellis Island as part of our immigration unit. We were reading all these stories about people in the 1800s coming from countries like Italy and Ireland and Russia to have better lives in America and we were supposed to ask our parents about our ancestors. My mom got really offended when I asked her. She said, "You know they came on a ship a long time ago."

"From where?" I asked, even though I knew.

"From Africa," she said.

We had to make presentations and she wouldn't give me enough information, so I just made up some story about this slave escaping from his master and then rescuing the girl he loved from a plantation. I got a poster and drew pictures and everything. I got a 10+ (in Peruskoulu, equivalent to an A++). A week later, the teacher said we were going to Ellis Island. The day before the trip, my mom gave me this long lecture about sticking with the teacher, being careful not to lean over the side of the ferry, going to the bathroom before we left the school. When she finally let me out of the car, she made me wait so she could hug me for a long time, as if I was going to another country.

I sat next to my best friend Reed on the bus, and we crowded in the back and sang "99 Bottles of Pop on the Wall" so loud that the driver pulled over and told us he would dump us out if we didn't quiet down.

After we reached Manhattan, took the ferry across the water, and reached Ellis Island, the teacher led us into the museum. They gave us a tour, where we saw the beds that the immigrants slept in and the rooms and all of that. After, we went outside to look at these gigantic rocks that had all the names of the people who passed through Ellis Island on them. My friends started looking for their ancestors, but I didn't because there wasn't anyone to look for, and the teacher saw me sitting on a bench alone and asked me if I was okay. I told her I was fine, though I desperately wanted to eat my lunch—my mom had packed some of my favorite foods, like a last meal before I went to the gallows.

"Look out at the water, Jordan," the teacher was saying. "Can you see Manhattan from here?"

I said yes; it was a blur, like squinting at a castle through the mist.

She leaned over me with her hands on my shoulders. "Can you imagine what the immigrants waiting to get to New York would have thought, standing right where we are, looking at Manhattan from here?"

And I thought that they might have been thinking, *Freedom is right over there.*

I told this story to Keira one day when I skipped school to go see her in rehab. Okay, yeah, I guess I shouldn't have skipped, but you don't know my principal so who cares, right? Anyway, we were at the hospital and she was sort of lying across my lap with her arms around my neck, telling me something funny one of the other patients had done; her shoulders were shaking because she was laughing so hard, and I tried to laugh too but it wasn't funny enough. I mean because of the situation.

"You're not laughing," she said into my shoulder. "Why aren't you laughing?"

I told her that I was.

"No you're not."

"I am. It's hilarious. It would be pretty cool if I could meet her, wouldn't it."

"No," she said. "No, you can't. She's not my friend, she's just some girl."

She started to talk about how she was not like the people in the rehab place, she didn't have friends here because they were really crazy, she was not like them.

I suddenly felt a rush of pity. "You're not crazy."

"I know I'm not." She sat up to look at me, and then pointed at a piece of paper taped above the window. "See that? I made that in art therapy. It's all black and shit, and blue and red and purple and green, and I didn't really know what I was doing, I was just making crap up to get points so I could watch TV at six with everyone else. You have to earn everything here like in school. So the lady came over to look at my drawing and said, 'Hmm, that's interesting,' and I'm like, 'Yeah,' and she says, 'Does this represent your chaotic mindset?' "

Keira climbed over my legs and got off the bed. "Like, what the fuck is that? *Chaotic mindset.* I said it wasn't supposed to represent anything but you know the way people look at you like they're nodding or something as if they agree but they really don't?"

She pulled the paper off the wall and brought it to me. Just as I reached out to take it from her, she crumpled it up, dropped it on the floor, and flopped down on the bed next to me.

"What's the matter?" I whispered.

She took a deep breath through the pillow and said she just wanted to get out of here.

I lay down so my face was level with hers. I said I wanted her to go, too.

"You shouldn't come here anymore. It's not…it's not good for you. You'll get sick soon. You'll start suffocating."

"Suffocating." I wasn't asking her to explain it.

"It's, it's like this crushing weight," she said. She started to cry.

I took her into my arms and kissed her, not in a romantic kind of way but the way a mother or father would. She didn't smell sweet like she used to. She smelled like ordinary soap and fabric, and that was even nicer than the sweetness.

"You're okay," I told her. "Breathe a little bit. You're not going to suffocate here, I promise. Shh, breathe a little bit," and I said this over and over again until she went limp and closed her eyes against my neck.

I rubbed the wetness off her cheek and stared at the walls. White color, clean paint. The window was locked or under alarm, I guessed. Gently I put Keira down on the bed and went towards it. When I pulled the latches, the interior part of the window opened, but the side that led to the outside was covered with a thick sheet of glass.

"I can't open the window," Keira said softly from behind me. "I don't have enough points for that."

I ignored her and reached up to unlatch the glass. The alarm started ringing but I pretended not to hear it; I unhooked the glass from the frame and put it on the dresser. Wind blew cold air and snow flurries into the room and Keira was there, sticking her arms out to feel the weather, and she was smiling and the cold was turning her pale cheeks reddish and she was putting her head through the window to remember how it felt to breathe again—

And then the rehab security guards with their uniforms and walkie-talkies and nurse sidekicks flooded in, surrounded us, and dragged us to some place called the isolation room, where they started interrogating us about the open window. I explained that it wasn't Keira's fault, and that I hadn't known we weren't allowed to open windows, and that when the alarm went off I didn't touch it again.

In the end, I walked away from that place and I was free, I had all my freedoms and I could go anywhere I wanted and watch TV whenever I wanted. She couldn't do that. She hadn't spoken during the interrogation, hadn't bothered to defend herself at all.

"Let him go," was what she'd said.

I wanted to say sorry but she looked too tired to bear it. When I got home, I opened my bedroom window and whispered her name.

Seriously, I don't even know why I did that. It wasn't like she was going to come or anything. Sometimes I'm such an idiot.

Oh lovely de Luna, beauty of the moon
The sun shines in the hall when I see you
And the heavens sing a lovely tune
And the black sky changes blue
If only you knew the love I have
These feelings in me are very new
Who knows what would come to pass
If you told me you love me too.
-Anonymous

Entry #8: Sanctuary

Sanctuary is being four years old and trying to open your eyes wider to find your father in the rain so you can keep following him, but too many coats look like his and you don't know who you're holding onto anymore. You stand there and cry, water soaking into your socks and school shoes. Hands lift you and tuck you within a jacket, against a chest. A familiar scent. Your father starts singing that old Madness song about rain falling on your face. You close your eyes. You're safe.

When Keira was little, her mom used to call her Keira-who-owns-the-moon. She'd hold her in her arms and sing to her in Gaelic. She sang the song to me in the car one time. It was late February when we were stuck in a freak snowstorm and I'd just turned fifteen. Keira had called my cell at like six saying she was outside. She said, "Up for a drive, Jor?"

I was vacuuming my room after weeks of my mom shouting at me to do it (I really can't keep any space clean, it's really sad) when she called. My family was going to eat dinner in two hours and my mom was pissed that I was leaving.

"You better come back before dinner," she said as I stuffed my feet in my boots and pulled on my jacket.

"I will, I promise," I said, kissing her on the cheek.

From outside the door, I could see Keira in the front seat. There were a few snowflakes falling then, but not storming like it would be later on. I got into the car, kissed her, and asked her where we were going.

She started the car and the radio turned on, blaring Nicki Minaj. "Nowhere."

A peaceful ten minutes went by without either of us saying anything, and then I started telling Keira about how my brother and sister and I used to sled down the hill on my block with all of our friends, and afterwards, we'd go inside and have hot chocolate and cookies. I asked her if she'd ever sledded before and she told me she used to do it with her friends when she was little but not anymore because she crashed into a tree. The other kid on the sled with her got hurt, and the kid's dad didn't let her play with Keira anymore.

"You know those people you used to be friends with way back when, and now you try not to remember their names?"

I said yeah anyway.

"It's like that," she said. Then softly she murmured, "Shitty people."

She went silent, probably turning over the bad memories in her mind, or suppressing them, or trying to reconcile. I changed the station to alternative rock. That was when the snow started coming down really hard.

"Hey," Keira said suddenly, "it's a winter wonderland."

She kept driving and we kept talking until we could hardly see through the windshield anymore. The wipers were useless; she parked at a random curb.

"So what do we do?" I asked her.

She suggested we go out and build a fort. An igloo.

I laughed and shoved her. "No, seriously."

She leaned away from the steering wheel and said we would just have to wait it out. I asked her how long she thought that would take.

"Twenty minutes, maybe."

I looked out the window. It was really dark and I couldn't see anything but the white flakes and patches of blackness. It was beautiful. The silence, everything.

We sat in the car for a long time, waiting for the storm to let up. Keira told me about her childhood, how her mom used to play with her all the time and bake cakes and tell her stories. She sang me a song about Connemara. Her mom used to push the tables and chairs against the wall and dance with her in the dining room. She knows all the words to "Come On Eileen", even though she doesn't like to admit it. She can also speak Spanglish, but she doesn't like to admit that either.

We told each other a lot of personal things that night, things even my best friends probably don't know, like how I sometimes feel like I have to be amazing like my brother and sister, and that sometimes I worry about my little sister, and that I worry about her too.

She said, "You shouldn't have to worry about me."

"What else am I supposed to do?" I asked her, and she laughed and told me I was too old for my age.

By the time the storm got a little better, it was almost nine-thirty and our parents had called us thirteen times combined and we were both exhausted. I was so comfortable, though. I was sad to have to get out of the safe, warm car to trudge through the swirling wind and snow to meet my angry parents at the door.

But anyway, it's what I think about when I see that word. Sanctuary. Keira and me inside, the rest of the world outside and far away. I dream about things like that on nights when I dream at all.

Phone Call from Nat to Jordan, 12/19/12

Nat: So how was the visit?

Jordan: It was okay. She didn't really do anything, just kind of complained and then cried and fell asleep on me.

Nat: What'd she complain about?

Jordan: Oh, like the food and the staff, but especially the staff, and like, why she shouldn't be there 'cause she's not an addict.

Nat: What do you say?

Jordan: Nothing really. I just kind of listen and say yeah, I know what you mean. Sometimes I don't know what to think. It's stupid, but sometimes I want to say, Keira, you're just in denial, and then sometimes I want to say, Keira, you're right, you don't belong here.

Nat: It's not your fault. You were thrown into it, you know?

Jordan: My parents keep telling me to break it off.

Nat: Well, they have a point, to be honest.

Jordan: Yeah, but you don't just abandon someone like that—you don't just leave when someone's made a mistake. I *know* her, Nat, that's the thing. I know who she really is. And when I see her I don't see drugs like everyone else, I just see *Keira*, the girl I love. Do you get it? I need to be there for her.

Nat: I just see you getting hurt by this, Jordan, and I don't think…you should sacrifice yourself for her right now.

Jordan: I'm not sacrificing myself.

Nat: You are. It's like, because she's suffering, so are you. Maybe I don't totally get it but I get that you have this devotion to her even though the situation makes you miserable.

Jordan: The situation, not her.

Nat: The situation *is* her.

Jordan: I was happy when I picked up the phone. I was happy before we started talking about this.

Nat: Are you crying?

Jordan: …

Nat: Are you crying?

Jordan: It's nothing.

Nat: Jordan, I can hear you. This is exactly what I mean.

Jordan: I hate you.

Nat: Don't cry, okay?

Jordan: I'm not.

Nat: Look, I'm really sorry. I shouldn't have said anything. Do you want me to come? I can bring some movies.

Jordan: Not today.

Nat: Okay, cool, I'm coming, then. Please don't cry, Jor, you know I didn't mean to make you cry.

Jordan: Can we not talk about it?

Nat: Yeah, we won't talk about it anymore, I promise.
         I won't bring it up.

Jordan: Good.

Nat: See you in ten minutes.

Jordan: Yeah.

(end of conversation)

January 2011

Freshman year, AP World History I. Slides of Phoenicia and Carthage. Close my eyes, picture Keira de Luna's face.

What I did was, I used a lot of Post-Its. And colored index cards. But mostly Post-Its. I wrote poems on them and slipped them through the cracks in Keira's locker. They were all anonymous, but she knew it was me, probably because I was so dumb as to not change my handwriting. It was the same as my signature on the literary magazine club sign-up sheets.

She came up to me as I was leaving the club room to wait for the late bus and said, "Hey. Freshie."

I didn't know she was talking to me so I kept going, and then she said, "Jordan Vianney."

"Oh," I mumbled, turning around, my face burning. "Sorry, yeah?"

"You're a Vianney, aren't you? Francis and Erin's little brother?"

"Uh, yeah."

She reached into her pocket and took something out. A yellow index card, folded up into fourths. She held her palm out flat, balancing it in the center of her hand.

"These notes are so stupid," she told me, but she was smiling and I could feel my heart bursting.

"S-sorry. I'm, uh, really sorry for—"

"You know what," she said suddenly, "you're pretty cute. You want to go out some time?"

I felt myself wanting to throw up, not out of disgust, but shock. "I thought you were…I thought you were going out with Andrew Hertzig."

"Andrew Hertzig?" She stared at me. "Why?"

"Um, well, he's kind of amazing-looking. And he's popular. And he's nice, I guess."

She laughed then. "You guess?"

"Uh, um, yeah."

"Then you guessed wrong, sweetheart. Andrew Hertzig's my lab partner, and I think you're way more amazing-looking, and nicer, than he is."

"Ha ha, eh, erm, thanks."

"So I'd like to go out with you. If you don't mind."

"No, no, I don't mind, in fact I'm actually very happy…I didn't think you would…I mean, I'd like to go out too. I'd love to."

"All right, cool." She smiled again and put the note back in her pocket. "Well, see you."

After that, I was in a trance. Keira was going to go out with me. We were going on a real live date. We were going out for dinner on Saturday night. It was raining, but there were rainbows and sunshine and flowers everywhere. I got a 68 on a math test but it was okay because I could do better next time, and who cared about geometry anyway?

I thought about her even when we were playing video games at my house. She was a distraction that kept getting me killed in the lamest ways.

We took a break to eat, and when Nat and Josh went upstairs to bring the juice, Audra pounced on me. Literally, she pounced on me and knocked me backwards onto the couch. She's overweight but in a pretty way, like I don't think she'd still be as pretty if she was skinny.

"Christ!" I yelled. My mouth was full of pizza pocket. "Audra, I have food in my mouth!"

"Jordan," she said, her face inches above mine. "Are you in love?"

"Get off me!"

"I can *tell*! Are you, are you?"

"No! Get off of me!"

"You're in love! Who is it?"

"Shut up!"

"Who is it?"

Nat and Josh came down with the juice and cups. Josh was like, "Whoa, guys, get a room!"

Audra raised herself up and I tried to get her off me and she grabbed my shoulders. We both fell onto the floor and Nat and Josh roared with laughter. I rolled away from her, got up, and sat back down on the couch.

"You crazy woman," I said, grabbing another pizza pocket.

"What's going on here?" Nat asked.

"Jordan has a crush and he's not telling me who it is!" Audra complained, like a tattletale.

"I don't have to tell you!"

"Then I'm going to guess!"

"Don't guess!"

She sat down on the couch and poured herself some juice. "Marie."

"Marie who?" said Nat. "Our grade or tenth?"

"The Marie in tenth grade has a really nice mouth," Josh said.

"Shut up, you guys," I said. "It's not Marie anyone."

"She's in our grade," Audra guessed.

"No. Stop."

"A sophomore."

"Stop it!"

"Junior?"

"Audra, I'm serious!"

"It's a junior!" she exclaimed.

Then the three of them started rattling off every eleventh grade girl, and then Nat said, "Is it Keira de Luna?"

And I was like, "No."

But Audra knew. "It's Keira de Luna!"

And I covered my eyes with one hand and buried my face in one of the couch pillows.

"Aw, you have a crush on an older woman," Audra cooed, rubbing my back.

"Do you, like, *know* her, Jordan?" Nat asked me.

I wanted to kill them all.

"She's not a crush," I said into the pillow. "She's my date."

The chaos started then. I shouldn't have said anything about the date at all. The three of them wouldn't stop acting so annoying around me, cracking dumb jokes, dropping stupid innuendos that didn't make any sense. They showed up at my door at nine on Saturday morning, ate breakfast with my parents, and ran upstairs to my room and jumped on me. I woke up screaming, thinking I was being attacked, and Josh had to clap in my face to shut me up.

"Are you READY!?" they all shouted.

"For Christ's sake!" I yelled. "Who let you guys in here, anyway?"

"We're here to prep you," Josh said. "You know. Your *date*."

So for the next eight hours, they fought over what clothes I should wear, what cologne I should put on, even what soap I should use. I was just going to wear jeans and a T-shirt, casual and whatever, with my black All Stars. Nat and Josh said I should wear a leather jacket, but Audra said no, I should wear a button-down with black jeans. She said, "You need to look professional."

"Professional?" Josh shouted. "You want him to look like a fucking teacher?"

They argued about this while I sat on my bed in boxers, watching *CSI: Miami* on TV. At five, I went downstairs to get some popcorn and met Nat on the stairs on my way back to the bedroom.

"You don't eat before you go out on a date!" he shouted. "You want your breath to smell? You want pieces of food to get stuck in your teeth? Frigging *popcorn* of all things!"

"Oh my God," I said. "Stop freaking me out."

They finally made a compromise. I was wearing black jeans, an Ed Hardy T-shirt, and a borrowed jacket when Keira rang the doorbell just as my phone received her text.

It took me a long time to open the door because my hands were shaking so much. Hers were in her pockets and her hair had been swept back, out of her eyes. When she smiled, it was clouds and rainbows all over again. How can the very sight of another human being make you so happy? Ask Keira, she's explained it. Ask her first and then ask me.

Entry #9: Luck

I think I might be a pretty lucky person. I mean, considering all the people who live in dire poverty or are being abused or are dying somewhere else in the world. I am probably one of the most naïve human beings on the face of the earth. I have never been homeless. I have never been beaten. I've never even been really badly bullied before. So what the hell do I base my Common Application essay on, then?

Maybe I should just write about my good luck and the fact that I have such a wonderful life. I mean, compared to most people. And I'm friends with a lot of people who have good luck, too. Like, Nat's mom got cancer when we were in sixth grade and our family was always over at his house and he slept over at my house a lot during that time. But she was really lucky because they were able to remove the tumors or something and now she's totally fine.

And this one time when I was thirteen, Aida and I almost got hit by a car. That was mostly my fault. Back then, I usually let her sit on my bike handles and then ride down the big hill that makes up part of our street. I'd take my feet off the pedals and then put them on the ground once the bike slowed down as it reached level road. Francis and Erin were always telling me not to do it, but Aida loved the thrill and nothing had ever happened to us until that day.

I'd just come back from lacrosse practice at school and I was dead tired and just wanted to eat, finish my homework, practice cello for my music exam, and play video games till midnight. I was eating some ham salad thing in my room and trying to do algebra when Aida burst in, all sparkly-eyed and out of breath.

"I want to go down the hill!" she said, jumping up and down and tugging my hand away from my fork and homework.

So I finally gave in, and she was so adorable and happy that I couldn't help picking her up and tickling her. I yelled into the house, "I'm taking Aida outside," and Erin shouted, "Don't go down that hill," but I didn't listen to her.

It was fine going down, Aida cheering and stuff, but as we reached the bottom of the hill I saw a car coming and I thought, *Oh fuck.*

I tried to move to the right, but when I did that, Aida fell off the handlebars. She had never fallen before. What was worse, there was a fucking car coming. She was screaming and I braked so hard that I literally flew off the bike and the stupid car was still coming, like coming right at her, and I crawled over to her and thought, *Well, whatever happens, I'll block her,* so I covered her like I was a fort and the car stopped.

"Oh my God," the lady said. "Are you kids okay?"

"Yeah," I said, but Aida was still screaming and screaming on the ground.

"What about the little girl?"

"She'll be okay."

And just like that, the bitch sped off.

I tried to move closer to Aida but everything hurt. I called to her. She ignored me. With a ton of difficulty, I pushed myself over and tried not to feel the pain. I pulled her closer to me and rubbed the bruise on her face and tried to wipe the blood off her knees and her elbow, but there was just so much and I was hurting everywhere and she kept on crying and it was all my fault. Seriously, when that car was coming, I thought we were going to die. Me and her. I thought we were done. But we were alive. And I didn't have my cell phone to call anyone, and I didn't think I could get up.

Aida buried her face in my chest and sobbed. She didn't seem to realize that I had actually caused her injuries. I patted her back and tried not to think, because then I would think about the pain and everything that came with it, and I'd freak out again.

After a long time of sitting in the road, I heard another car coming, and I finally forced myself to stand. Aida was still whimpering. She wanted me to carry her. I took her hand and made her walk. I didn't have the strength to carry her or my bike; I left it on the curb.

Erin and Francis flipped when they saw us. It was a good thing my parents weren't home because we were all beat up and bloody, and Erin said, "You went down that damn hill and you fell, didn't you?"

I started crying. Francis told me to be quiet and take a shower before our mom and dad got back. I told him my bike was still outside and he said he'd go get it. While I was in the shower, Erin cleaned Aida up at the sink and yelled at me for not listening to her. She said, "That's what happens when you think you're so smart even though you're just a stupid kid," blah blah blah, and I just went on crying. Later on she took pity on me and decided not to tell our parents. To this day, they still don't know.

When I'd come out of the shower and dried myself and plastered Band-Aids all over my cuts and bruises (and I had many of them), I told them what had happened.

Francis said, "You know, you should be grateful for all your good luck. You don't even really deserve it."

I've said that before too, when Keira and I were on her bathroom floor and I was kneeling on the tiles, holding her hair back while she puked in the toilet and moaned.

"I'm going to stop," she told me then. "This shit's making me sick. I'm sick, Jordan. I'm going to stop."

"Please," I said. "What if you overdose?"

She didn't care. She told me I didn't need to worry about her OD'ing, that it would never happen. I didn't really answer that, just kind of nodded, and started washing the vomit out of her hair. There was sweat all over the back of her neck and shoulders. I looked at myself in the mirror, I didn't recognize anything I was seeing.

Phone call to Jordan Vianney from Erin Vianney, 11/15/12

Erin: So I heard you got into a fight at school.

Jordan: Oh, did I?

Erin: Yeah. Francis told me.

Jordan: So Francis goes and tells you but he says nothing to me. Wow.

Erin: Stop trying to change the subject—

Jordan: I wasn't even trying to change it.

Erin: Is it that hard to listen to anyone say anything bad about her?

Jordan: He wasn't just saying stuff, that's the thing, he was being insulting.

Erin: So you punch him?

Jordan: Well, he shoved me!

Erin: What you mean to say is, "Well, he was talking shit about Keira so it's okay that I punched him, if it's for Keira."

Jordan: You're so mean. Why are you being so mean?

Erin: I'm not being mean. You need to hear it from somebody. This is getting out of hand.

Jordan: What is.

Erin: Your love life. It's not healthy, Jordan, not for you and not for her.

Jordan: How is it not healthy for her? Should I break up with her when she needs me the most, is that what will make her all better?

Erin: I just want *you* to feel better.

Jordan: I'm fine.

Erin: You're going around punching people! How is that fine?

Jordan: Don't you have better things to do than to yell at me?

Erin: Stop talking. Listen to me.

Jordan: Okay.

Erin: When Francis told me, I thought he was talking about someone else. I didn't even recognize the person he was describing. Is this who you want to be?

Jordan: No.

Erin: Well, this is you as Keira's boyfriend.

Jordan: (mumbles something incoherent)

Erin: What did you say?

Jordan: It's really late, I'm going to bed.

Erin: Tomorrow is Saturday.

Jordan: I have detention, I'm waking up early.

Erin: I want to be angry at you, Jordan.

Jordan: Then be angry at me. I'm angry, too.

Erin: At yourself?

Jordan: Myself. You. Her. Everyone.

Erin: Don't be mad at me. You know it's only because I love you.

Jordan: I know.

Erin: Do you think Keira loves you?

Jordan: Yes.

Erin: Like the rest of us love you?

Jordan: …

Jordan: I don't know.

Erin: If you don't know, then—

Jordan: Erin, I'm sorry but I really have to go.

Erin: All right. I'll talk to you tomorrow.

Jordan: Bye.

Erin: Good night.

(end of conversation)

Entry #10: Stress

In health class last year, we did this thing where the teacher told us to close our eyes and picture ourselves on a beach or whatever. He'd be like, "The waves, the waves are coming, crashing and rolling. You feel the cold water. You feel the warm sand."

I forget what it's called, something about imagery, but he was trying to get us to understand stress management. I misunderstood. I thought of it as hypnotism, the yoyo swinging back and forth in front of a person's face. You're getting sleepy, you're getting sleepy.

It was stupid. I thought, *This would never de-stress me.*

We also learned about eustress and distress. Eustress is like, I guess, happiness or something. Adrenaline, I think, which is a sort of stress but instead of being terrible, it gets you excited and gives you energy. Distress is the bad kind of stress that can cause heart disease and low immunity and so on.

The teacher gave us this project to do: we had to make presentations on our own forms of stress management. I used a tri-fold only because I didn't know what else to use. I printed out pictures of headphones and pillows and bicycles. I taped on a photo of the lacrosse team, shots of my friends and me making stupid faces and holding up peace signs. For each one, I wrote a long, overly-detailed paragraph about the significance of this kind of activity. Relief, relief, relief. I used that noun over and over again, so many times that it even began to annoy me as I gave my presentation. The teacher gave me a 100, which was not deserved, because my entire project was based on lies. I don't *have* stress management techniques. I just don't. I don't think a lot of people do either, that's why so many Americans are depressed and sick and obese and suicidal.

Dr. Scheinberg says I need them. She suggested I do yoga or something. I used to do that with my mom in the mornings before preschool, and it was held at the top of this building across from a park. The instructor and all the other women thought I was so cute and were always carrying me and giving me treats and telling me I had such great form. Back when I was flexible.

When I was twelve or thirteen, my sister Erin would do these sun salutation things she found in *Seventeen* magazine. She tried to get us all to do them with her, but only Aida was willing. While I sat slumped at the table at seven o'clock in the morning and drooled into my cereal, my sisters were out on the lawn stretching their arms, doing yoga on mats laid out on the grass. From the window, through my half-dead eyes, they looked like they belonged in some fitness DVD with the tan, smiling instructors. Erin said it helped her start her day and made her more energized. I told her there was shower gel that did that. Francis said she should drink some coffee. She just laughed at us and said the sun salutations were liberating, just like the Ladies' Night Outs she and Aida and my mom have on Friday evenings.

My dad's always like, "Hey, the girls are gone, let's turn on the TV and find a game and watch it together, us manly men, ha ha ha."

It isn't funny. And I hate watching sports on TV, they go on for hours and make my butt fall asleep. Our Guys' Night Outs are supposed to be "releases of the week", to de-stress ourselves and become more connected as father and sons. But he and Francis usually sit in front of the TV screaming at the Giants or the Knicks or the Islanders while I watch *Lost* on Netflix in my room and only go back downstairs to get the jar of cucumber and lime preserves and a spoon.

To be honest, I'd rather go with my mom and my sisters and fall asleep watching some shitty chick flick in the theater than watch those stupid games with my dad and brother. I mean, at least if I went with them to the movies, I'd be able to get free food or something.

But I don't think I can like, ever fully *relax* by doing the same activity over and over again. It's like taking medication. The only time I ever chill out completely is when I'm hanging out with Nat and Josh, or Damian and Jess and Kennedy (my friends from lacrosse, which I'm not allowed to play anymore), which I rarely do anymore. Now I just go home and lock my bedroom door and all the stress stays inside.

First time I saw you I was

Forever invisible

Little kid chasing after lacrosse balls over the hill, I

Saw you by the doors

The way the color in your hair caught the eye of the sun

The way your cheeks glowed under the trees

The way you stood there like an impenetrable force,

Forever invincible

Forever in my memory.

-Anonymous

ENTRY#11: DEATH

Your heart stops. It pumps like that dog in this book I read when I was a little kid, about this boy who runs the Iditarod in Alaska or something to win money for his sick grandpa. The dog was going so fast that its heart couldn't keep up and it stopped altogether, right at the finish line. Just like a person. The heart stops like that.

That wasn't how Fortinbras died, and I kind of wish he had died like the dog in the book, because at least he'd have been doing something he loved. I don't know why I really care about that, considering he'd been so terrible to me, but at least it wouldn't have been as painful for him. But Fortinbras was hit by a car towards the end of sophomore year and Audra wouldn't talk and Nat and Josh and I stood around awkwardly, waiting for the whole thing to be over. We tried to make her happy. We brought her to our houses, made her cinnamon rolls, square-danced in straw hats and high heels to make her laugh, rented her favorite movies and watched them with her in my basement. Like I said before, we also had a funeral, but she didn't show up because she just couldn't handle it, I guess. The dog was like her baby. She'd wash him in a basin in her backyard, making sure the water was warm, scrub his fur with a brush, and moisturize it with some diluted lotion. Fortinbras had a dog house but he always slept at the foot of Audra's bed, curled up in the animal version of the fetal position. He had a bunch of different collars to match Audra's outfits. It was weird but sort of cute, in a bizarre way.

So she missed him a lot. And she was so unhappy, no matter what we did. It was when we were square-dancing for the second time that she finally got tired of us. She didn't want to laugh or play games or eat badly-baked pastries. She wanted to go to Ink Plaza.

No one said anything. We just looked at her. Then Nat said, "All right, let's go," and we all got into the car. The three of us guys wanted to talk about the weirdness of Audra wanting to go to Ink Plaza, but she was right there, leaning out of the window with her hair nearly blowing into all of our mouths, so we exchanged confused looks instead.

We waited outside for her (because she told us to, not that we wanted to, but we could see her clearly through the big glass windows so it wasn't too bad) until she finally came out. Her eyes were bloodshot and she smelled metallic, like machinery or a handful of coins.

"So," Nat said, and Audra held up her right arm. *Fortinbras* on the inside of her wrist, written in thick black Shakespearean script.

"Shit," I said, because I thought what she'd done was stupid, especially considering the fact that her parents are super strict and would kill her if they found out about it. But you know, she's my best friend. I helped rub ointment on her tattoo and bandaged it and told her it was a nice tribute, because I love her. You just have to do those kinds of things. When Nat's mom was sick and he was coming over a lot, there was this time his mom passed out or something and the ambulance had to get her. The Starkleys live on my block but all the way down and around the bend or whatever, so I could see the ambulance zooming down the street from where I was playing video games in my room.

Twenty minutes later, my mom said, "Jordan, Nat's mom is sick and the ambulance just came to take her to the hospital."

My mom said she was going to the hospital to see if there was anything she could do to help Nat's dad. My dad said he was also going, and told Erin to look after us. Aida was in bed already but she woke up because of all the commotion and the three of us sat in front of the TV in our parents' room watching *The Lion King* with Aida spread out across all three of our laps, sucking her thumb. We'd almost finished it when my mom came back. She shouted for us to come down, and Erin picked up Aida and we all went downstairs.

"Nat's sleeping over," she told us, holding him in front of her with her hands on his shoulders. "I'm going to go back to the hospital. I'll come back soon, okay? Erin, take care of everyone."

She kissed all of us, including Nat, and put Aida to bed again. I wanted to ask Nat about his mom but I didn't want him to get upset, so I said, "Let's go to my room."

We played video games until Erin came in and told us to go to sleep. I went into my bed and Nat lay down on the blowup bed. We were mostly silent, not really talking about anything. I was starting to close my eyes when Nat asked me not to fall asleep. He started talking about how when people fall asleep, nobody wants to wake them up when something bad has happened. I told him he shouldn't worry about things like that, but then he was crying and telling me I didn't understand, his mom was going to die and he would be asleep and he wanted to at least be able to say goodbye and say he loved her.

"She looked really bad, Jordan, really bad," he sobbed, and I wanted to do something but I didn't know what to do except to call Erin, and when I suggested it, he said no.

"She's going to be fine," I told him.

"You don't know that."

I got off my bed and squatted next to the blowup bed. "She will, Nat."

"You don't know. She looked really bad."

He was covering his face with his hands. I wanted to pull them away and hold them. Instead I hugged him and let him cry into my shoulder, and I could feel his tears in my chest—his crying was making *me* want to cry. I mean, I hated seeing him like that. He's my best friend.

I let go of him when he told me he was tired. I said he should go to sleep, and I went back to my bed and lay awake listening for his deep sleep breathing. We both fell asleep. And he didn't wake up until morning. And his mother didn't die.

ENTRY #12: GUILT

Okay, so as a little kid, I was spoiled as hell. I don't mind admitting this. I *was*. Because for five whole years I'd been the baby of the household until Aida came along with her constant crying, and my parents gave her constant attention (especially my mom, who I was very clingy to at the time). Maybe I felt neglected? I would always try to do stuff to make my mom look at me; read a book at the top of my voice, do a cartwheel on the kitchen floor, hit my brother, anything.

There was this time I was in second grade and we were doing this concert at school, and I got chosen by the music teacher to sing "This Old Man" only because none of the other boys in my class had memorized the lyrics yet and I was still in rock star mode back then.

The same day of the concert, my mom had to go for a business conference in Philadelphia. She'd been telling us about it since the week before, but I was too busy practicing in front of the mirror and recording my singing voice on my dad's cell phone to pay much attention to anyone. I was standing on the stage under a warm pink spotlight, already in the middle of the first verse, when I realized my mom wasn't in the audience. It was just my dad with the video camera and some of my cousins.

My mom came back the next day. I refused to speak to her because I was so angry, and she tried to explain to me over and over again that she had told me she was leaving and she knew I'd sung wonderfully and she was so proud of me, but I couldn't bring myself to forgive her. Then, because she was tired of my antics, she got pissed and told me to leave her alone. The next day, I decided to run away.

I'd mapped it all out Kevin McCallister-style. I put on my jacket, stuffed my feet into my Spiderman rain boots, packed my suitcase, and left the penthouse. I just like, left. Erin and Francis were watching TV in the living room and I went through the kitchen and unlocked the door. I had thirty dollars (back when I used to receive an allowance) and I used some of it to buy a Metro card for the subway and a pink and blue paper box of stroopwafels from this bakery near the apartment building. The old guy, his name was Bel, he was from Hungary. When I came up to the counter, he was like, "Where's your mother today?" and I was like, "She's got the flu and I wanted to get her some stroopwafels so she'll feel better."

He smiled and lowered the price. I ate two on the subway and got crumbs all over the lady sitting next to me.

The adventure was great at first, even though I'd forgotten my gloves and scarf and my nose was running. I felt like I was starting the rest of my life, like I was a grownup and I could live by myself and not go to school and eat pizza and cake all day.

So where was I going to do all this pizza-and-cake eating?

At the Plaza, of course. I'd seen it a thousand times, and once, Erin, Francis and I had gone in with our mom so she could use the bathroom. That was it. I thought, *Wait till I tell them I stayed at the* Plaza Hotel.

It never occurred to me that I needed more than twenty bucks to pay for a room. When you're a little kid, that's a lot of money. Now it's like nothing. You can barely buy a decent shirt with twenty dollars. You can't even buy any nice shoes. I didn't know that then, and when I finally got to the hotel and stood at the counter, staring up towards the ceiling to see if maybe my eyes could find a face, the hotel concierge lady bent over and looked at me like she was seeing a creature from outer space.

"How may I help you, young man?" she asked me.

"Can I please have a room?" I held up the money but the counter was pretty far away. "One with a view?"

The lady took the money and looked at it. "How old are you?"

"Seven," I said. "And eleven months."

"Lucky you, to have a birthday next month," she told me. She gave me back the money. "Where are your parents?"

I made up some bizarre story about my parents moving to Belize and leaving me at the Plaza because I caused too much trouble. In the end, the lady made me give her my parents' phone number (she actually threatened me with the police if I didn't!) and I sat on the floor and cried all over the candy bars the hotel staff gave me while I awaited my parents' arrival. Even as I was waiting over there and crying, I couldn't stop moving—fidgeting, wiggling my feet, shivering. They were going to kill me. They were going to *kill* me for what I'd done. My brother and sister were going to hate me for trying to run away. I wondered why things always worked out for Kevin and Matilda and everyone else, but not for me. I figured there was power in being on TV, power we normal people didn't have. Something about the fact that we're real and they're not, maybe. And then I looked up, and my parents had come.

My mom ran over to me and picked me up and hugged me so hard I thought some bones were breaking.

"Oh, sweetie," she said, and her voice was shaking, and soon I could feel something sliding down my neck and into my shirt collar. Tears. Warm tears. My mother was crying. It was like a bomb had exploded inside of her and I'd set it off, but instead of sparks, there were her tears.

"I'm sorry," I told her. "I'm sorry, Mommy."

She forgave me eventually, and I got severely punished for that stupid little stunt. That was the first time I remember ever feeling guilty about something. It was nearly ten years ago, but sometimes when I look at her, I remember what I did and how I made her cry and it just kills me. Memory is sometimes a killer.

FEBRUARY

Today we're going to retrace Holden Caulfield's steps around the city and I am not excited, reason being that I actually was planning to ditch school today until Mr. Dowling said the field trip (and the packet that comes with it) costs twenty percent of our grade. It was a wonderful piece of blackmail. My participation grade is dragging my English average down to an eighty-nine, and twenty percent looks huge on paper.

The bus is so fucking hot that it makes my nose hurt. I slip down the aisle, moving between giggly pairs and silent pairs and bouncing pairs— Nat and Josh together in the back and Audra with some loud, obnoxious stage crew girl—until finally I find an empty seat in the back and scoot close to the window. Nice, cold glass. I plug in my ear-buds and listen to my Yanni playlist, but I can barely hear anything over the sound of Mr. Dowling's voice. He's sitting in front of me, going on about how *The*

Catcher in the Rye is supposedly all about society and the fight against superficiality, "Holden is the truth among a bunch of hopeless liars," he is saying to the art history teacher, and, "blah blah blah, I can quote a real life author, I am so the coolest shit."

He is not the only one who thinks so. He has a cult following. Vera Jergen and all her people sit around in English class and accuse the rest of us of being phony, call the media phony, call reality TV phony, call the government phony. Call their mothers phony. Who gives a crap about what all of us think? Who gives a crap about what Holden thinks?

All of us, apparently, for today. The bus dumps us near Grand Central Station, our starting point, where we stand at the top of the stairs and listen to Mr. Dowling read a section of the book to us. I am in the back again, alone and unable to hear. He can't see me inching near the café nearby and handing money to a cashier in exchange for a bagel and some orange juice. By the time I've shoved the receipt in my pocket, he's finished.

"Okay, kids," he says happily, "are you ready to work those leg muscles?"

Everyone groans except me because I have a bad headache, and plus, I'm eating.

He says, "I'm going to separate you guys into groups of two," and I hate him for his optimism. I hope he forgets that I exist.

He doesn't forget. He partners me with this girl I don't really know, which somehow works out because she actually doesn't know me either. She's new and arrived last month from California, and she's not even paying attention to what's going on, she's just taking pictures of everything with this awed look on her face like she's seeing the pyramids at Giza, or something equally astounding. She doesn't see me. We move on.

At every stop, Mr. Dowling reads us a section of the book. We are on Fifth Avenue but I can barely hear him above the wind and my own sniffling (runny nose). I think about moving to the front but I don't want to be so close to all those people. Instead, I decide to pretend that I know what he's saying, and stare up at the icicles hanging from a store roof, counting the drops of water that keep coming off and making small holes in the mounds of snow on the sidewalk.

"Hey," my partner, the girl, suddenly says, "can you even hear what he's saying?"

"Not at all."

She laughs. "Me either. It doesn't make a difference anyway. It's not like he's telling us anything new."

"I know, right?" I turn to get a better look at her. "Hey, you're new, aren't you? Elizabeth?"

"Yeah. Jordan, right?"

"Yeah."

She looks up at the icicles, breathing with her mouth open, like she's never seen those things before. When she catches me staring at her, she blushes hard and looks away. "Sorry. I, um, moved here from San Diego."

"It's okay." I kick at the snow. "What was it like in San Diego?"

Elizabeth is taking a picture of the icicles on her iPhone and she doesn't hear me. She's standing on her tiptoes. Shiny white Doc Martens, skinny jeans, and a white trench coat. Her style kind of reminds me of Reed's.

"Oh my God," she says when she's done taking it. "Everyone's going. We have to hurry and catch up."

I look ahead and they are all the way down the street. "Whatever."

"Come on, we have to go."

"We don't have to go."

She looks at me with puzzled eyes. They're like these stones we got on a field trip when I was little, they were made of tree sap. Amber.

"We don't have to go," I repeat. "We can go somewhere else and catch up with them later."

"But wouldn't we get in trouble?"

"No, dude. I swear, he won't even notice we're gone."

Elizabeth spends a long time looking at her phone. Then she finally looks up. "Sorry, I had to Instagram that. Where are we going first?"

"Wherever. Are you hungry?"

"Yeah, I guess."

"We can get some food."

"Okay."

"You want to see my old street?"

Her eyes almost fall out. "You used to live in Manhattan?"

"Yeah. You want to see where?"

"Yes!"

I buy a metro card for the two of us and we get on the subway. My apartment building, which I myself haven't seen in a while, hasn't changed much, and my old school, Peruskoulu Steiner, has changed drastically (it's now better-looking on the outside, and bigger).

As we walk past the building, I show her the candy store I used to love so much. The Hungarian guy's gone, which makes me feel kind of sad inside, like a piece of me is missing.

"I used to go here all the time," I tell her, wandering aimlessly through the aisles. It feels like there are flames being lit on my eyelids. I take off my new glasses and rub the lenses on my sleeve. "I miss being a kid."

Elizabeth picks up a bag of chocolates. "I bet Holden misses it, too."

"Holden's selfish." I move on to the hard candies. Aida's been asking for one of those gigantic swirly lollipops.

"I think you said that in one of the class discussions."

"I did?"

"Yeah."

"Oh. Yeah."

"What's so selfish about him?"

"I don't know, he's just flunking school after school and his parents are paying for it, you know. And they want him to do well. And other people want him to do well, but all he thinks about is how phony the whole world is, and there's nothing he can do about that so it's all just a waste of time. You know what I'm saying?"

"I know what you're saying."

"I just think he's hurting himself and other people."

Elizabeth takes a picture of a row across from us. "What are you looking for?"

"Something for my sister."

"How old is she?"

"Eleven. She's a sixth grader."

"Cute." She puts her phone back in her jeans pocket. "Hey, are you okay? You look kind of sick."

There's a stabbing pain in my right eye; I take off my glasses again. "I'm fine. I'm going to pay for this and then we can go."

I buy the lollipop and two chocolate bars and we leave the store. I give her one of the chocolate bars and get us both coffee. Mine's black as hell, like I could literally fall in and disappear in it; I usually fill it up with milk and sugar, but for some reason I'm really feeling horrible and don't know if I can stand the combination. I take tiny sips and nod and smile, dazed, as she talks about school and her old school and Mr. Dowling and how annoying he is.

"He is annoying," I say. I put my head on the table and close my eyes just for a little bit. When I open them, there she is, hair falling over her forehead, saying, "I think you're sick."

"I am," I admit, unwillingly.

"Why?"

What a weird question, I think. *Why?* "I don't know, I guess stress?"

She puts her hand on my face like my mother would have, had she been there. "Ooh. Hot."

"Hot?" I laugh. "Are you sure?"

Elizabeth laughs too. "I think you're also becoming delusional. Come on, we better get back, it's almost two. Drink your coffee." She grabs me and we leave the café, huffing and puffing in the cold, cold air. The weather makes my nose hurt again.

"Don't hold my hand, it's all sweaty."

"It's good, Jordan. You're supposed to sweat out a fever."

And she keeps holding onto my hand.

Underground at the subway entrance, she adds money to the metro card and we get onto the subway. She talks the whole way there, about her mom and dad and older sisters. She says she used to take ballet but her teacher started criticizing her all the time, telling her she needed to lose weight and stuff, so she quit. We sit side by side and look out the window, making little comments about the darkness and the lights and the smell of New York City underground. She lets me put my head on her shoulder.

"I had fun today, Jordan," Elizabeth says. "I really did."

"Yeah," I tell her. "I did, too."

"I'm sorry you got sick."

"Me too."

Later on, Elizabeth falls asleep against the seat, and I think about how nice she was. I think about the other kids and how we are all so different now. I guess that's how the world works, though. I guess I can't blame them. Maybe if I was in their shoes, I wouldn't hang out with me either.

ABUELO MAKES ME FEEL
BY KEIRA DELUNA

Harborhill Friends High School Literary Magazine, 2012, pg. 19, "Staff Prose"

Say you are sixteen years old, and you are exhausted.

Abuelo's bedroom door is closed and the cousins are snoring in the living room, and your aunt is putting away tortillas in the kitchen. You can't sleep. Your NyQuil's run out, you'd taken the last of it the night before, trying to get to sleep with all the people in the house. Abuelo wanted to die in his eldest son's home since he couldn't go back to Mexico, since his kids wouldn't let him.

You remember him saying, *Quiero morir en la casa de mi nacimiento,* and you always passed by the room and thought, Well, that's a beautiful way to do it: in the house you were born in. Dying with all your former selves.

But you can't sleep because you keep thinking about this time when you were five and you were afraid of a thunderstorm and your grandfather carried you outside and stood on the porch with you and said, *Mira, mijita,* the rain is beautiful, and stretched your hand out so the drops would collect in your palm. It's not the things we're supposed to use to fall asleep (but doesn't this say Ambien?), not the pieces you're familiar with, someone else's. A mistake they didn't think you'd touch. Another dream. You're tired and you can hear your father crying in his bedroom and nothing matters anymore.

You don't fall asleep. You stay awake feeling wonderful because you can hardly feel your body, it's almost like it doesn't exist, you're floating in your bed and the darkness around you is a supernova. When you dream that night, you dream about astronauts. You kiss your boyfriend in outer space.

It's called *cristal*, Google says, and you have the diamond in one hand and a glass of water in the other, squinting at the screen. Abuelo's diamonds make you feel him.

They make you.

Crush, with this Hillary Clinton paperweight your dad gave you for Christmas, scoop *cristales* into a line, forget about the things they told you in grade school, inhale, inhale, as you watch the moon change phases.

Abuelo makes you feel. Are you so high your feet don't touch the ground? So wasted that you're body disintegrates? So stoned you've become a fucking rock?

No, it is discovering that his own footprints can lead you to heaven.

Entry #13: Friendship

I have a lot of friends. My theater crew (there are really too many people I'm friends with in that place; the Depth Crew's like a big gigantic family, so I'm not naming them), my team, kids in my classes and in clubs and afterschool activities. But they're not who I tell my problems to; they're not the ones whose shoulders I cry on. Not that I do that anyway, but I mean like, if I did. That kind of thing is reserved for people like Josh and Audra and Nat. Well, it used to be. I don't really talk to them anymore. So maybe I should say I *had* a lot of friends. Now, it's Erin kind of, and Joni and Reed and Elizabeth.

Reed is, no offense to all my other good friends, the greatest friend I have. He was probably my first ever friend. We've been best friends since we were three. We went to Peruskoulu Steiner together but after I left, we stayed in touch. His sister was actually the second person I ever kissed, the first being my friend Joni (also from Peruskoulu Steiner), and that was in third grade at Mariner's Gate. But I was nine and she was eight and a half, and it wasn't anything real. We'd actually been inspired by *Spiderman*, MJ and Peter's upside-down kiss scene. I was Spiderman, hanging upside down from the monkey bars, and Joni was MJ who'd just been saved, and I closed my eyes and she stood up on her tiptoes to kiss me with her hands on either side of my face.

"You taste like salt and vinegar," she said when she decided to let go.

"Yup." I'd just finished a bag of potato chips.

And that was it. We ran around the jungle gym for half an hour and then went off to find Joni's mom so she could take us to get brownies like she promised.

When I kissed Reed's sister, we were thirteen, the summer going into eighth grade. Our parents made us apply to this program where the chosen kids stay in a historical city and learn more about the country and leadership and whatever. We tried to protest against it because we wanted to spend the summer doing nothing, and we'd be wasting two whole weeks in another state with a bunch of nerdy losers, we said. Reed's parents were going to give up on it, but my mom had a talk with them about it, and then they made him go. Reed's parents tend to listen to a lot of the things my parents say because my parents are like a thousand years older than them; Reed's mom was eighteen when he was born and his dad was twenty-four. They're divorced now, but anyway, we went to Boston that year and had a ton of fun despite all our complaints about nerds and stuff.

The very day we came back, Reed took me with him to his sister's house in Bayside. She's his half sister (his dad's daughter) and is six years older than him. She was turning nineteen and they were throwing a backyard barbecue party for her. Nina (that's her name) is funny because she always acts like her brother is such a nuisance but really she loves him with a passion. When he braked too hard on his bike, fell off, and sprained his arm in Washington Square, she flipped and blamed me and gave me the evil eye for at least three years after that. The day of her party, we were done with that hostility, and she just hugged me and talked about how big I'd gotten. After that, Reed and I escaped to go play with the kids and eat food and stuff, and then Nina randomly came up to me and was like, "Thanks for being such a great friend to my brother. I really appreciate that." And she kissed me. On the cheek. But Reed likes to joke that she gave me my first kiss, even though I guess it was really Joni.

It was annoying at first but then I stopped caring. What I mean to say is, he can be pretty annoying but we all love him. He's like a twin brother even though we're like opposites. He has that sort of over-the-top personality that usually aggravates me when it belongs to other people: loud, outgoing, talks too much. He's fun as hell, but a terrible study partner because he loves distracting you from your work. Your trig final will be the next day and you'll say, "What the fuck, the quadratic equation isn't working and neither is factoring," and Reed will be like, "Hey, did you hear Eminem's new song?"

If you say no, he'll turn it on and play it for you. If you say yes, he'll turn it on and play it for you. If you ignore him, he'll start laughing because he knows you're ignoring him because he's being annoying, and his laugh is super infectious.

Elizabeth reminds me of Reed sometimes. I hang out with her a lot now. I mean, I still sit with my usual group at lunch, but I feel like a corpse, sitting there with no one to talk to, not saying anything because if I do, everyone will look at me like I'm a convict. It wears the fuck out of me. And Elizabeth and I don't have the same lunch period. So we sit next to each other in English and history, and we drive to school and back together in my car. I can't exactly describe her; all I can really say is that I like being with her. I don't know, she makes me happy. She makes me forget about things like time and Keira and all the staring. It still hurts to see Nat and Josh and Audra together somewhere, like if I'm going to the movies or driving home from school with Elizabeth or walking down the hallway. They probably think about the old times too, just like I do when I'm alone in my room and it's dark and I'm listening to all those pop songs we used to sing along to in middle school.

But they have each other anyway, and they're done with me. They're done because I took too long to be done with Keira, and they've worked too hard to let their reputations come crashing down with mine, and they don't know how to believe me anymore. They moved on, which is a good thing. It's just me who hasn't.

April 2012

There was only one play we were allowed to perform in the school, and that was *The Silver Skates*. I read the abridged version of the book when I was younger so I already knew the story. It's about this boy named Hans Brinker and his sister Gretel who live in the Netherlands and are really poor because their dad is brain-damaged from an accident he suffered at work like ten years before. Then this really nice doctor, Dr. Boekman, does surgery on their dad for free after the dad tries to shove the mom into the fireplace (he's delusional from his head injury). Because the doctor did the surgery for free, Hans can buy nice skates for his sister and himself with the money he saved. And then, of course, with new skates they can participate in the race to France or wherever.

Kai wanted us to actually do it on ice. He wanted to try to get people to come to the community rink to see it, and so he made us practice there. For forty-five minutes, we'd skate in a circle while Kai shouted, "Around! Around! Smooth! Smooth!" from the stands. I literally fell down a thousand times, not because I lost my balance, but because other people lost theirs and grabbed onto me for support even though it's not like I'm big or anything. And once this girl named Rachel bashed her head into the side of the rink and she was knocked out for three seconds. Everyone was freaking out, and Alec and I volunteered to go with her to the ER, but Kai made her walk it off and keep going. We started calling him The Dictator and plotting the overthrow—Alec, since he was bigger than Sadie and me, was supposed to tackle him from behind. Once he was on the ground, I'd jump on his neck and Sadie'd blindfold him. We'd lock him up in the janitor's closet and tell everyone he'd hit the road back to Hilo. But then our advisor showed up at the rink as we were getting ready to execute our plan and saw what we were all doing. He was like, "Where's Kai?"

Somebody said he was buying coffee. The advisor went out to get him. We could hear them arguing outside the doors.

Kai couldn't accept the fact that he couldn't put the play on ice. He made phone calls and wrote letters and complained every two seconds. He even made me and this other kid stand in the main hallway and hold up posters in protest. I didn't really mind, I was willing to do it for the art, as Kai said, although I didn't know whether we were trying to target the administration or the student body. Unfortunately, on the second day of protest, my brother saw me and said, "What the fuck are you doing, Jordan?"

And without bothering to explain, I said, "Kai made us do it."

And my brother went to Kai and was like, "If you're going to choose a kid to hold up one of your stupid posters, it better not be my little brother."

Kai rolled his eyes and said, "Yeah, yeah, your goddamn reputation."

But he gave up on the fight after nobody returned his phone calls. The case was closed. We were performing onstage.

My character didn't actually exist. Kai made him up. At first I was really upset by this, because usually when parts are made up for you, it means you were so bad that you couldn't play any of the other roles.

"That's not it, Jordan," Kai told me. "You're unique. I had to make you a unique character. I want to challenge you."

So I was Anselm van Piet, a thirteen-year old orphan in love with Gretel, who was this girl named Vera Jergen. I was never really friends with her, but she's in some of my classes and she's one of those smartass people who randomly tells you her GPA and how she takes AP everything and cries when she gets an 89 while you sit there and hold your 52, wanting to strangle her. Because

Anselm is in love with Gretel, Vera and I were supposed to kiss. I was like whatever, but Vera made a big fucking deal about it.

"I don't want to kiss someone else," she whined. "I have a boyfriend."

"Jordan has a girlfriend," Kai said, "and you don't see him complaining."

"That's 'cause he's a guy. He doesn't get it."

"Yeah, I didn't want to kiss you either," I said, and then Kai told us to shut up.

Whenever we practiced, Vera would kiss me with her eyes squeezed shut and I'd do it with my nose scrunched up. It was just a little peck, no biggie, but she still complained about it to her friends, which was extremely irritating.

In regards to the kiss scene, Kai pointed at me and said, "You look like the Soviet." To Vera he said, "You look like the United States."

"Why the fuck am I the Soviet?" I asked.

Vera was like, "I can't be the United States. My GPA is a 99.6 un-weighted."

Kai said, "Jordan, that was an insult. Take offense."

Then I had to stop my scrunching. And Vera had to stop her squinting. Kai suggested we pretended we were kissing our partners, but at the thought of that, I nearly barfed (there was no way I could convince myself that Vera's lips belonged to Keira) and Vera became really offended by it (though I really hadn't meant to offend her—you don't control your vomit triggers). She almost bailed on the play altogether, but the three of us worked out a compromise: Kai would give me money to buy zucchini muffins from the school café and he would get Gretel nicer outfits to wear. After that, we were okay. We practiced the scene. We were good.

The only scene that was not so good was the part where Anselm's mother dies and he bursts into tears on her lifeless body and has a total nervous breakdown. Kai kept telling me I was too stoic. When I tried not to be stoic and emphasized the weeping noises, he said I was being fake. My tears were forced and took too long for me to produce; he criticized them too.

"You need to summon Pain with a capital *P*, full-out tears and bawling," he told me.

Pain with a capital *P* was not my forte. I didn't know emotion like that.

I watched sad movies like *My Sister's Keeper* and *The Notebook* to try to force myself to cry, but *My Sister's Keeper* just left me depressed and I fell asleep after forty minutes of watching *The Notebook*.

"Dead puppies," Kai said, with his hands on my shoulders, looking directly into my eyes.

I pictured dead dogs. I thought about the road-kill I'd seen on the bus ride to school and got grossed out all over again.

"Dead mother."

But I couldn't muster the image. My mother, dead? Impossible.

He sighed. "Okay. Okay, I know you don't want me to talk about it, but, um. Think about Keira."

"No," I said.

"Jordan—"

"Kai. No."

"No?" he asked me. "Are you being serious, Jordan? How serious? How serious are you, Jordan, huh? Huh?"

And I said, "Shut the hell up," and he said, "Can you imagine what would happen if she told you she loved drugs more than you, if she breaks up with you because you're just standing in her way?"

I wanted to hit him but instead I started screaming for him to stop talking, and he grabbed me and whispered it in my ear again, slower this time, and I shoved away so fast that I fell down and landed on some hard, sensitive bone in my butt.

"Jordan," Kai said, and I was breathing a lot, trying to catch my breath while at the same time trying not to look at him because I didn't want to cry.

"Jordan," he said again, and I inhaled deeply and said, "What."

"Are you okay?"

"Yeah." And then I gave in to the crying, because I wasn't okay at all and he'd hurt me and Keira might hurt me and also my ass felt like it was broken.

He squatted down next to me and watched me cry. He leaned over and hugged me.

"I'm sorry, dude," he said. "I didn't mean it. You know I didn't mean it, right?"

"You didn't have to do that."

"I know I didn't. I won't do it again. I'm sorry."

I rubbed my eyes with the heel of my palm and wiped my cheeks with my hoodie sleeve. I missed Keira. I wanted her to hug me so that I could press my face into her clothes and breathe in the smell of her detergent.

"Fuck," I said. "Whatever."

He promised me he'd get me a brownie, and I almost started crying again because I remembered Keira standing at my front door with a plate of warm brownies covered in chocolate sauce and strawberries on my fifteenth birthday, singing a song we'd heard on the radio, and I just missed her so fucking much it was unbelievable.

"Is this Pain?" I asked Kai after a few minutes, and he cracked a small smile and shrugged.

We didn't say anything about it, but I thought it was. I didn't use it in the play, though. I couldn't do that just for a character in a show. I guess that's why I'm not such a great actor. I can't give pieces of myself away.

January, 2011

Parties. Even before I entered high school, I'd heard about the parties. Scandalous hook-ups, illegal drugs smuggled in by a friend of somebody's foreign cousin, and gallons and gallons of booze. There were guest lists for these parties. There were waiting lists for these parties.

Some people were so popular that they weren't on any lists; they were automatically expected to come. Like Erin and Francis and Kai. And Keira.

"I'll pick you up on Friday and we'll go together, okay, love?" she said with her face pressed against the side of mine, her lips brushing against my ear.

"Uh, okay."

"Or do you not want to go? We don't have to go if you don't want to. We can go somewhere else."

It was late January, but I wanted to go to the outdoor mall where this local band would be performing, and dance in the square under the snowflakes.

"No, I want to go."

"You sure?"

"Yeah."

"Great," she said. "I can't wait to show you off."

She turned and walked back to her car, leaving me at my front door to stare back at her and not know what to make of the weather. Because for the first time in my entire life, I had to worry about shit I'd never cared about before, like what clothes I should wear, if I should put on Axe or nothing, or if I should tell my parents I was going to a party with a bunch of juniors and seniors I didn't even know. They were already starting to get suspicious; I kept walking back and forth from the bathroom to my bedroom, and supposedly I was only going to Josh's house.

I got the Axe from the bathroom, went back to my bedroom, shut the door, and called Nat.

"Dude," I said, "I'm having a crisis."

"Is it serious, man? I'm playing *Grand Theft Auto*."

"Yeah it's serious! What the hell am I supposed to wear?"

He sighed and told me he'd come over. In a few minutes he was searching through my closets, throwing clothes on my bed, and yelling at me to try stuff on instead of sitting there playing Wii. Nat was awesome though, because soon I was wearing a cool outfit underneath my thick winter jacket and standing against my dad's car, shivering in my combat boots. It was really dark and I wasn't wearing gloves because I didn't want to look like a dork.

"Jory-Jor," Keira said, coming out of the darkness to kiss my forehead. "You look great. You want to go now?"

"Sure."

We got into her car and she cranked up the heat. She wasn't seventeen yet so she wasn't supposed to drive at this time of night, but neither of us cared. It was the usual.

When we reached the house, I could already hear the music coming from the stereo inside. Katy Perry, Kanye West.

"Who's house is this?" I asked.

"Jensen."

"Jensen Ross?"

"Yeah, him."

I hardly knew who Jensen Ross was, except that he was a senior and he'd once dated my sister back in middle school. All the people here, I knew their names and faces but I didn't *know* them.

"Doesn't matter," Keira said. "They all know you."

This, I realized, was partially correct; she led me around like I was her equal, which I definitely was not, and when she introduced me as her boyfriend, the other kids would say, "Oh, this is little Vianney, right?"

"Jordan," Keira would correct. "He's Jordan."

There were coolers and shots and things, but Keira got sodas for both of us. Ryder Jung came out of nowhere and was like, "Hey, Jordan. Keira, you don't want a beer?"

"Nah, not tonight."

Not tonight? I thought. *Does that mean she usually drinks at parties?*

For some reason, I found that incredibly cool.

"What's the problem, man?"

"Nothing. I just don't want to drink."

As she and Ryder were talking, I turned my head to look around the room. The place was dark and packed with people. Some of them weren't even from our school. Some of them were Harbor Hills Friends alumni. And Jesus Christ, there was my brother standing against the wall with a red cup in his hand, talking to some guy while his girlfriend was all over him giving him a hickey. Francis was drinking! It was perfect blackmail material.

"Come on, Jordan," Keira was telling me now. "Let's go dance."

I didn't really want to, especially not in front of all those people, but she grabbed me by the arm and pulled me to the center of the room.

"Just look at me," she said. "There's only me and you and Flo Rida. Just dance."

And so it was just me and her and Flo Rida, and then Chris Brown and Ke$ha and Beyoncé, and there was a circle of people around me shouting, "Little Vianney! Little Vianney!"

And I wanted to tell them all that my name was Jordan, and that no, they could not compare me to that Latino dancer from America's Got Talent, but then someone yanked me out of the spotlight and dragged me through the crowds of people, outside into the cold.

"What the *fuck* are you doing here?" Francis shouted at me, waving his arms in the air like a freak.

"Hey," Keira said, stepping through the door. "Francis, what's the problem?"

Francis swirled around. "Keira, why would you bring him here? He's only fourteen years old! If you get him laid or hammered or anything, I'll kill you, hear me? I'll just fucking destroy you."

"Chill out, Francis, you're drunk."

My brother turned away from Keira and looked back at me. He looked back at Keira.

"Take him home," he said. "Now."

"No, I want to stay."

"You," Francis said, leaning over to meet my eyes, "you shut your damn mouth and get out of here before I tell Mom."

"So tell her, then. Let her see you all drunk and hickey'd up."

"Go to hell, Jordan, little bitch. You hearing me, de Luna?"

Keira put her hand in her jeans pocket and took out her keys. "C'mon, Jor, let's go."

Fifteen, I thought irritably. *I'm fifteen now, not fourteen.*

I stomped angrily through the thick snow to the car. I didn't care about leaving the party— that wasn't it. It was Francis and the power he thought he had over me. I hated him.

Keira caught my arm and put her fingers through the spaces between mine.

"It's okay," she said gently. "It's late, anyway."

"Yeah, I guess so."

The car smelled like strawberry jam and her hair. I said, "You usually drink, Keira?"

She smiled, and in the dark she seemed to be blushing. "Well, I mean, sometimes. When occasion calls."

"Oh." I leaned against the window and closed my eyes. Keira hadn't wanted to drink because I was with her. Because someone had to drive me home, I realized.

"You could've had a beer and Francis could've driven me back," I told her.

"I could've," she answered, "but he was drunk today. And anyway, you're *my* baby."

Hers. Me.

Wow, I thought to myself, watching the snow fall outside. She thought about me beforehand. She thinks about me. *She thinks about me.*

"This isn't the way to my house," I said, looking through the window. "You have to turn back."

"We're not going to your house," she told me.

"Then where are we going?"

"To the mall," she said. "We're going to go dance again."

I sat up to look at her, trying to read her. Had she known? Had she known all along?

"Why are you doing this for me?"

She leaned over past the steering wheel and kissed my forehead. "Because I love you, silly."

So we went to the mall, where the band was still performing in the square, and we danced under the snowflakes in the freezing cold. And I swore I would remember that forever.

ENTRY #14: HOPE

A fluffy white thing with angel wings. A word with feathers.

Back in tenth grade when Keira was in rehab and I was all supportive, I had hope. I looked up the Twelve Steps and read books about addiction: *Tweak*, *A Million Little Pieces*, *Crank*, *Beautiful Boy*. I loved Nic Sheff's honesty in *Tweak*, but my favorite was his dad's, *Beautiful Boy*. I blew all my money buying new copies of the books I'd read for her and left them on her nightstand with *Beautiful Boy* on top, saying, "That one's the best, Keira."

She didn't read any of them. I sat by her bed and tried to read them to her. I wanted to help. She said, "I don't want your help."

"You don't want it?" I'd repeated.

"I don't need it," she told me.

I made her playlists. She didn't like them. She didn't like anything. She was dealing with the side effects and it was bad, really bad. She'd tell me about it, how she wanted to peel off all her skin and couldn't eat anything and puked all the time. Withdrawal, they called it. They gave her medicine and stuff too, I guess to help her with the withdrawal, but nothing seemed to help.

"She has to get worse to get better," the nurse told me. She was this really nice chubby lady who had a weird accent and gave me chocolate caramels.

"Maybe she won't want to go through all of this again so she'll just decide to stay clean from now on."

She said, "It's all up to her."

"Yeah, but what can I do?"

"Don't put her sobriety upon yourself," she said. "It's not your job to take care of her like that. You come here every day, sweetie. Don't you leave any time for yourself?"

"But I love her," I told her.

"And she needs to love herself if she ever wants to stay clean."

When the nurse said that, I felt my eyes start to water like I'd just been hit in the face. I mean, why did Keira not love herself? *I* loved her. I loved her so much that I'd lay awake at night thinking about it. Why couldn't she try?

Every day after school, I came to remind her. I told her she was beautiful. I sang rock songs to her in my crappy voice. I played the guitar and stroked her hair and kissed her even though most of the time her lips were chapped and tearing.

"Keira, I love you," I said, over and over again. "I love you, I love you. I want you to get better."

"Jordan, baby," she said, "you don't even know what that means."

That hurt me. "Read *Beautiful Boy*," I told her. "I'm going home."

Then I left. But of course I came back the very next day.

OCTOBER 7, 2012

In October, we went to this amateur filmmaking ceremony in the city after "The Rebirth" won sixth place. They were honoring us with a banquet, and as the producer and director, Kai came to the school from Princeton on Friday to tell us that we were all going to meet in front of the Astoria, which was where the banquet was being held.

I went with Sadie, Alec, Jonah, and Emiline, some of my Depth Crew friends. We rode the train together and took the subway to the hotel, where a bunch of kids from our school were already waiting in front of the doors.

"Where's Kai?" Alec asked this girl named Miranda.

"I don't know," she said. "Late, as usual."

I bought myself a smoothie from a street vendor while we waited for Kai to show up. He finally came, all decked up in a tux and shiny dress shoes.

"Hey, kids!" he exclaimed. "Let's go!"

All of us got checked off at the entrance to the ballroom before we were allowed to go in. It was almost like those movies where the kids try to sneak into a concert, but a huge bald security guard stops them and asks them for their names on the clipboard he's holding. The only difference was that we were VIPs. It was totally sweet.

The ceremony was only a ceremony for about twenty minutes, when they announced the winners and gave out the framed certificates. After that, it became one gigantic party.

Kai deserted us to go make connections with famous filmmakers and we sat at the table with our fancy expensive steaks and baked Alaskas, not knowing what to do. I mean, what were we supposed to do? We were a bunch of kids in a room full of like, Academy Award-winning producers getting drunk on champagne. I wanted to fall asleep on top of my soggy risotto, but then my phone started vibrating in my pocket.

"Take it outside," Alec suggested, so I left the room and picked up.

It was Keira. She'd been out of rehab for a week already but we were broken up, so why the hell was she calling me?

"Hey," I said in a cracked voice. "What is it?"

She was crying. "I miss you. I miss you, Jor, so much."

"Well…" I didn't know what to say. I shifted the phone to my other ear. "Well, you're done with rehab so you should do stuff again. You know, go back to school and hang out with people and whatever."

"What people?"

"Your friends, Keira."

"And you? You're not my friend anymore?"

"I'm not your *boyfriend* anymore."

"I didn't mean it, okay? I love you. I'm better now. I love you so much. Please come see me. Come right now."

I sighed. "I'm actually pretty busy."

She started crying harder. "Please come, Jordan, I don't know what to do—it's like I want to get high but getting high isn't enough anymore, I just want to stop feeling things, I just get so overwhelmed sometimes you don't even know how fast do pills kill you not fast enough right what about burning but isn't that too painful Jesus what am I saying to you just tell me to shut up God I wish I could just shut up please come Jordan I love you I want to see you I've been wanting to see you since forever I'm sorry I'm sorry I just want to die I'm sorry for all the shit I've—"

"Okay, okay, shush, it's okay, I'm coming."

"You are?"

"Yes." My heart was pounding. I could taste the risotto at the back of my throat.

"When?"

"Right now. Stay on the line, okay? I'm coming *right now*."

There wasn't time to tell everyone I was going, I thought, and plus they'd probably yell at me. *You're broken up, don't forget that.* I hadn't forgotten. She wanted to die.

I raced to the subway, gasping into the phone, constantly going, "You're there? Are you still there?"

I bought my ticket at Penn Station and waited until eight for the track number to show, and then I rushed onto the train and sat next to the window. The cold of the glass was calming. I huffed and puffed into the phone. "Keira, are you there?"

"I'm here." Her voice was soft, so breakable.

"Are you home?"

"Of course."

I heard the beeping of incoming texts but didn't bother to check my phone. She hadn't spoken for a while. "Hey, you still on the line?"

"Yes." She sighed. "I'm here waiting for you."

The taxi to her house from the train station cost me thirty-five dollars. Keira's car, which had been in the driveway unused and untouched for months now, was the only one in front of the house. When I rang the bell, she answered it.

"It's really you," she said, reaching out to touch me. Then she put her hands on my shoulders. Then she held me close, so close that our chests pressed against each other and I confused her heartbeat for my own.

Her mom was asleep, she said, and her dad had gone out. We were in her room listening to music. We were outside on the porch, tracing leaves on pieces of paper. We were everywhere and silent. She didn't speak.

"Are you tired?" I asked her.

"Mm-hmm."

"Then go to sleep."

"Later." She looked over at me. "Are you tired?"

"Yeah." Very. I was lying beside her on the covers of her bed, blinking and trying to stay awake. The truth was that I was exhausted. I was going to pass out. I passed out in my tux and hosiery-shop socks, deaf to my ringing phone and blind to the world outside of my dreams.

Fucking dreams. She was there, she was rising and sitting on the side of the bed, she was holding something shiny and extending her arm, blue and green veins crisscrossing underneath olive skin that had stopped glowing a long time ago because she started sighing too much, just as she sighs now so she wasn't cold like I thought she'd be because it's funny you think they'd be cold but she'd retained much of her original warmth she was still just as beautiful as ever I thought to kiss her how long had it been I'd held her in my sleep, felt her shaking, thought it was only because she was having a bad dream and this too shall pass was she not breathing then either I saw some stuff some drugs heroin coke maybe crack maybe molly mixed with a little blood there on the nightstand I thought to scream finally when her father hit me it was okay I didn't care her mother hit me in the face screaming, there was this explosion of pain and blood, I couldn't feel anything not even when they said get out of this house and I didn't know what else to do maybe leave them alone I took my phone but I forgot my shoes and jacket and my god her eyes weren't closed that was the scariest part they were rolled up like a zombie in a cheap movie yet still so beautiful goddamn what am I thinking now what the fuck was I doing then I only needed to run somewhere to the train station again I guess? She was shaking. elisa was there magic she tutors in the bronx I think she said WHAT HAPPENED TO YOU WHERE WERE YOU YESTERDAY WHY DO YOU LOOK LIKE THAT I looked insane probably with no shoes I realized I looked down my feet realized I couldn't see out of one eye, but my feet the bottoms hurt my lungs hurt my eye fucking hurt I said jesus Elisa she's dead and it's my fault I just sat there she said WHAT WHAT THE HELL WHO ARE YOU TALKING ABOUT I said I was so tired so damn tired but shit I was going to get arrested and they should arrest me because I did it and there's such a thing as being guilty of doing nothing in school they teach you not to be a bystander like when someone gets bullied see something say something I saw I love her I love her with all my soul I was just too tired it was like in a dream she was shaking she was grabbing me that's what I was thinking of and where did she get it where the hell did she get it well I don't fucking know. I don't.

I went to reeds and he said holy crap you look like shit why I told him can I come in he stepped aside and I just broke

Session : 24, 3/10/13

Dr. Scheinberg: Do you want to know what I think about this, Jordan?

Jordan: What.

Dr. Scheinberg: I think the root of the problem lies in your insecurity.

Jordan: And why do you think I'm insecure?

Dr. Scheinberg: Or perhaps you feel insignificant?

Jordan: In what way?

Dr. Scheinberg: You're always talking about New York City. You must like being here a lot.

Jordan: Yeah, but how—

Dr. Scheinberg: You don't value yourself in the suburbs because everything is so uniform. You are unable to maintain an identity.

Jordan: What?

Dr. Scheinberg: That's why you hold on to Keira de Luna, isn't it? Because she makes you feel important?

Jordan: *What?*

Dr. Scheinberg: So you disagree.

Jordan: Yeah, I do.

Dr. Scheinberg: Then why do you think you may be insecure?

Jordan: I'm not insecure.

Dr. Scheinberg: Hmm.

Dr. Scheinberg: Have you ever heard of the term 'generation wasted'?

Jordan: No.

Dr. Scheinberg: It's a noun describing a group of people from a certain time period who are quick to fall under the influence. A result of the previous generation's experimentation with drugs and other related paraphernalia.

Jordan: ...

Dr. Scheinberg: Do you understand this definition?

Jordan: What previous generation.

Dr. Scheinberg: What I mean about the previous generations is that they became pathways to accessibility.

Jordan: Okay, so...

Dr. Scheinberg: So first we have the group of young people before World War I, and then World War II, and then my generation, 'the scientists'. 'The scientists' were the experimenters. They were the hippies and activists and revolutionaries who came up with the weed and drug culture of the sixties and seventies. And now, ever since the late eighties, there has been 'generation wasted'. Your generation.

Jordan: Yeah.

Dr. Scheinberg: Kids like Keira, Jordan.

Jordan: …

Jordan: The adults are always criticizing us. They say we're spoiled and we get everything handed to us. They say we won't be able to love our own children.

Dr. Scheinberg: It's a possibility.

Jordan: You know, when I look at the clock behind you, I don't know how to read it.

Dr. Scheinberg: What?

Jordan: I mean I forgot how.

Dr. Scheinberg: What are you talking about, Jordan?

Jordan: Whose fault is it, then, that we don't know how to love properly?

Dr. Scheinberg: …well, the young people of today are plagued with issues that previous generations don't know how to deal with.

Jordan: When you love people you want to give them everything.

Dr. Scheinberg: Please, elaborate.

Jordan: Me, I'm not insecure. I'm going to love my children the way my parents love me. Maybe more than that.

Dr. Scheinberg: Do you think your parents have made mistakes, Jordan?

Jordan: Yeah. But so have I.

Dr. Scheinberg: And do you think you're a good son?

Jordan: Well.

Jordan: I'm not wasted.

If we see the sun and Juliet is the east
then you are the universe's shining heartbeat.
-Anonymous

July 19, 2011

The summer I was going into tenth grade, Keira got a job as a lifeguard and I signed up to be a swimming instructor at the community pool. It was a coincidence. One day when we were at this Italian ice place she asked me, "What are you doing during the summer?"

"Teaching swimming," I said.

"Awesome!" she exclaimed. "I'm going to be a lifeguard!"

We weren't in the same section. I was in the kiddy pool coaxing three-year olds to wet their faces and Keira was on the other side of the center, sitting high on a beach chair with a whistle around her neck. Sometimes I could see her if I stood on the steps, but otherwise, we didn't see each other at all. The only times we did were when we had our lunch break and went somewhere to eat together. Usually after the break, I'd go back into the locker room to get my towel again and Keira would return to her lifeguard post.

There was this one day Keira forgot her towel and borrowed mine, and she was nowhere to be found when I'd finished the lessons. All the swimmers and instructors were gone by then and I needed to dry off and change, so I decided I'd go to the ladies' locker room to see if she was there. The kids were still afraid of the water and I was dying of dehydration, so I was in a pretty crappy mood.

I knocked on the door and when no one answered, I opened it and looked in.

It was so random, Keira in there kneeling behind a bench like she was praying over the Eucharist, using some kind of thick green straw to breathe in a line of white powder on a gum wrapper. I didn't know what I was seeing at first.

"Hey," I said.

She looked up at me with the straw still to her nose, not even bothering to hide anything. "Yeah, Jordan?"

Her voice was level, as if it was so fucking normal for me to enter a locker room and find her sniffing drugs on a bench. My face started burning. "Um, what are you doing?"

"It's nothing."

"Is that meth?"

"No. *No*, baby, no way." She got off the floor and came over to me. "I would never take that. Hell, I don't even know where I'd get any of that."

"Then what is it?"

"What's what?"

"That stuff you're taking."

Keira sighed heavily and ran her fingers through her hair. The rubber band that had been holding it back into a ponytail snapped out and fell in a circle of pool water on the ground. She stepped towards me and put her hands on my shoulders.

"It's nothing, Jordan," she said again. "Just medication."

"So you're taking prescription meds."

She hesitated. "Yes."

"Prescription meds that were not prescribed for you."

She dropped her hands. "It's not like that," she said.

"Then what is it like, Keira? You're on drugs, and I was right before. When I found them in your pocket, I was right."

"I was barely taking them then."

"So you were taking them."

Keira sighed again. "Crap. Baby, don't cry. Don't cry, okay? I don't take any more than I'm supposed to. It's just one. One a day. I have to snort it so it works faster."

"Why do you need it at all?"

She put her hands on my cheeks and wiped my tears away. She held my face and brought me close to her chest. "You don't get it."

Her skin was wet and soft and smelled like baby sunscreen. There was a reddish sunburn on one shoulder; she'd gotten it last week and I went over to her house and sat on her bed, rubbing the ointment in. But I wasn't supposed to stay with her. I was supposed to end it because she'd lied to me and hid things from me and snuck around behind my back and she was an asshole and she was *addicted to drugs so I had to break up,* and then she said, "You don't get it, Jor. These things help me."

Her lungs were so close to my heart. I could feel them expanding, her breathing.

"You're addicted," I whispered.

"No. I'm depressed. These are like antidepressants."

I took a shivery breath and struggled to look back at her. "You're depressed?"

She looked away. "Something like that."

"I depress you?"

"No! No, Jordan. No, you make me better. You really do. I just want to be better for *you*. I want to be happy so you won't be sad. I mean, I see when you get upset because I'm upset. I just hate when that happens."

I stooped down to pick up the rubber band. I wiped it on my swim shorts and moved her hair back.

"Don't tell anyone," she said. "Please."

I put the rubber band around my wrist and wrapped it three times so that it pressed into the skin and left an indentation. "If you stop."

"I'll stop. Don't tell anyone."

"If you stop, I won't."

"I will." Keira put her arms around me and her silky hair fell down over my neck, tickling my bare back. "I swear to you, I will. Don't cry anymore, Jordan. I love you. Don't cry anymore."

She cleaned up the powder and put the straw (actually a rolled up fifty dollar bill) into her jeans pocket and asked me if I wanted to come to her house to have dinner, but I couldn't. Not in front of her parents. Not when I knew something about their daughter that they didn't know. I told her and she said she understood.

She dropped me off at home and I went straight to my room to lie down. My cell kept ringing, all different numbers, people wanting to hang out with me. I couldn't face anyone without wanting to tell, because I needed help and I was scared and I'd never dealt with something like this before.

Isn't this dangerous? I asked myself. *Haven't people died from drugs?*

It was all in her head. But I trusted her, didn't I?

I do, I thought.

So I kept her secret. And I hated myself for it.

MAY 16, 2011

We were in the school parking lot and it was morning, and she was talking about getting her nose pierced.

"I think your dad will murder you," I told her.

She laughed. "Maybe he doesn't have to know."

"Are you honest-to-God serious right now?"

"About what?"

"About getting another piercing."

"Well, yeah. I mean, I want one. I always wanted one."

"People are going to think you're badass." I was joking but she took it seriously.

"Yeah, I know," she said, shoving her hands into her jacket pockets. "They'll judge me and stuff. They'll think I'm like, a gangster's girlfriend. Ha ha ha."

I smiled and played with one of her hoops. "When are you going to do it?"

"Saturday. Will you come?"

"Yeah, I've got nothing else to do." I took my hand away. "Just kidding. I'll come because I love you."

She came early on Saturday and I took a long time to wake up and get dressed, so she'd already finished eating breakfast with my parents and my sisters before I came down.

"Where are you guys going today?" my mom asked.

Keira began to blush, and I said, "We're going to Stefani's house."

"Stefani Spinelli?"

"Yeah, her."

"Okay," she said. "Tell her parents I said hello."

And we were off, just like that.

"We are Kick-Ass and The Bitch Slap," Keira said, starting the car.

I messed with the CD player, swapping Sublime for Maná. "Who's Kick-Ass and who's The Bitch Slap?"

"Today you're Kick-Ass. Also Tuesdays and Thursdays."

"What about Sunday?"

"Sunday we take our break." She switched the music to a Bob Marley CD. "Fasten your seatbelt, kid. We're going to Jamaica."

Meaning the avenue, but we sang reggae the whole way there.

The piercing place looked like a hair salon and the inside smelled like nail polish remover. I sat on a revolving chair and played games on my phone while the ear piercing guy pushed Keira's hair back.

"Nasty-looking scar," the guy said.

I sat up to see. There was a dark reddish blotch that was only slightly visible at her hairline but seemed to continue down her scalp.

"Yeah," Keira said. "Gruesome stuff."

"How'd you get it?"

"Dirt bike racing. I fell off and hit my head on the track."

"Crap, that must've been painful."

"Yeah, it was." She smiled smugly at me and I rolled my eyes.

The guy wiped the side of Keira's nose with alcohol and said, "All right, sweetheart, you ready?"

"Yeah."

I scooted closer to her salon chair so she knew I was close by, just in case it hurt or something.

"Don't say one two three," Keira said. "Just do it."

She didn't make a sound when the needle went in; she just squinted a little and grabbed my hand and that was it. There was a small red hole above her nostril and the piercing guy put a stud in it. She let me touch it in the car.

"You have to twist the stud around," she told me. "So it doesn't close up, or whatever."

"Does it hurt?" I asked her.

"Not really. Sort of."

"Did it hurt when you fell off your...*dirt bike?*"

She laughed and swatted me. "Shut up."

"How did you really get that scar?"

"I was running and I fell."

"My sweet, lovable spaz."

"Well, when you're running really fast on the sidewalk and your foot suddenly hits like a rock or something, you're going to fall and slam your head on the ground."

"What were you doing, playing a game?"

"Not really."

"Then what were you doing?"

"Running from a dog."

"What, was it chasing you?"

"Nah, it wasn't even moving. I was just scared."

I had to turn my face so she wouldn't see me laughing and get offended. She said, "Jordan, I can *hear* you."

"I'm sorry. I'm sorry. It's just so funny."

"I was a little kid."

"Are you still afraid of dogs?"

"I wouldn't *run* from one."

We drove in some silence until she said, "I'm going to hide my face with my hair. That way, no one will say anything about the hole."

"Unless you wear a hoop," I told her.

"Pssh. No hoops. Everyone would think I was some Latina hoodlum if I wore one of those."

"Yeah, but who cares about what people think of you."

"Honey," she said, "judgment is the juror with the son who doesn't wear earrings."

"And what the hell does that mean?"

"It means people look at you based on how they look at themselves."

"Okay, yeah, what does this have to do with you?"

She pulled at the tip of her nose, maybe because it was hurting. "Everything, Jordan."

Later that night, Keira's dad found out about the piercing and grounded her. And I went out at dawn and snuck into her house through the basement window she left open for me and tiptoed upstairs to her room. She was sleeping. God, she was not a girl, she was an angel. I sat on the bed and watched her chest rise and fall.

"Forget about the judgment," I said, even though she was asleep and deaf and miles away from the present. "Don't think about things like that. Please, Keira, stop thinking like that."

I sat there next to her warm body for a few minutes, wanting to write a note or leave her a letter, but I felt like if I left a note I was asking for something in return. So I decided to just go home.

FIGURES BY KEIRA DELUNA

Harborhill Friends High School Literary Magazine, 2011, pg. 12, "Staff Prose"

My room.

You say, Smells like hazelnut, which is maybe what I smell like

You are light kisses and falling flower petals, but I don't say it out loud,

just that I like words and I write them on my walls and I like you

I have written on your arm before, you say it tickles, because I use felt-tipped markers

Abyssopelagic, Halcyon, Catachresis, Aegis, Elegiac.

I remember that you are young when you ask me what abyssopelagic means, it is the layer right above the ocean floor, and when I was a little kid I thought I'd touched it but turns out it was just the bottom of a swimming pool.

I don't explain.

I wait for you to speak.

You talk about how cool it is to be passionate about something—what are you passionate about, love? Your cucumber and lime jelly?

Songs and movies, too. The cucumber and lime, he says, is even better if you eat it with your fingers, your hands will smell like summertime, tangy and cool, like a curtain over your tongue.

You are touching my things. I hate when people do that, but you are not real, you're an illusion of space, a shard of infinite time: inexplicable, like us and faith.

"Well, you."

You like songs and movies and cucumber-lime jelly. And me. I want to write *me* on your arm, I want to fall into your dreams and keep on falling, stay asleep so we never grow up.

Live among the notes you sent me: parts of us I can't bring myself to throw away.

Phone Call from Catherine de Luna to Jordan Vianney,
9/20/11

Jordan: Mrs. de Luna, hi, how is everything?

Mrs. de Luna: Everything is fine here, sweetie, how are
your parents and your brother and sister?

Jordan: They're doing well, thanks.

Mrs. de Luna: Listen, I don't mean to bother you, but
have you noticed Keira acting, er, strange lately?

Jordan: What do you mean by strange?

Mrs. de Luna: I think...I think she may be taking drugs.

Jordan: Wh-why...how did you...uh, did you find any?

Mrs. de Luna: Yes.

Jordan: Um.

Mrs. de Luna: I was putting away some laundry and I
found, in her drawers, empty prescription pill
bottles.

Jordan: Um.

Mrs. de Luna: Did you know about this?

Jordan: No.

Mrs. de Luna: I didn't think you did.

Jordan: ...Mrs. de Luna...please don't cry...

Mrs. de Luna: I'm sorry Jordan. You're such a good boy,
and I don't know what happened to Keira...I have
to tell her father and I don't know how I'm going
to do it. I don't know how to confront her about
this, either.

Jordan: I, um, I can help.

Mrs. de Luna: I don't want to do that to you.

Jordan: No, I can help. Really.

Mrs. de Luna: I'm sorry Jordan, I don't know what happened.

Jordan: Please don't cry, Mrs. de Luna, she'll be okay. She'll be okay, I know she will.

Mrs. de Luna: Oh, sweetheart, I'm so afraid, but yes. I know she'll be okay, too. You're such a good boy. Let me not spoil your evening, honey. Say hello to your mother for me.

Jordan: I will.

Mrs. de Luna: Don't worry about this. Sleep well tonight.

Jordan: Everything will be fine.

Mrs. de Luna: Yes. All right, well, good night, sweetheart.

Jordan: Good night.

(end of conversation)

Entry #15: Pretending

When I was very little, my mom used to take me everywhere with her—to the store, to her friends' houses, to that yoga place—while my brother and sister were in preschool. She said I used to talk to things, like if it rained, I'd ask the sun to come out and stuff like that. I used to have these boots that made me a superhero during the day, and in the night, I'd arrange all my action figures around my bed because the moon gave them special monster-killing powers so they could protect me while I slept.

That was what got me through the summer going into sophomore year. I literally forced myself to believe that when Keira was angry for no reason, screaming at me for not showing up on time and getting nauseous in the car, it didn't mean she was withdrawing. That, when she was outrageous and random and full of this shallow, excited energy, it didn't mean she was on something. I would lay awake at night and go over these things in my head. No, it wasn't that. No, she said she'd stop. She promised me. She was okay. She made a promise. She has never broken a promise before.

I tried to erase all the parts where she'd lied to me. I made it so that they just didn't exist anymore. After I did things like that, I always felt so much better. I stopped asking her to quit and trying to confiscate the drugs and threatening to tell someone. That made me feel better too, which is really sick, but that's how it was. It kind of took the responsibility off me. Like, if you don't know there's a problem, what are you supposed to do about it?

But then her mom found out, and then it was fall. Cold and windy. When I came to the house, the car doors were open and her dad was carrying suitcases.

"Hi, Mr. de Luna," I said, holding up a hand.

He smiled sadly at me. "Keira's in the house. She'll be glad to see you."

God, I didn't want to see her. I had failed her.

I walked up to the house and felt Keira's cousins' eyes on my back—*they knew they knew they knew.* The little girls stopped and waved, remembering me from Keira's birthday parties. Did they know why they were here? Did they know why their cousin was leaving this morning?

I opened the door and went in. Women and men were swarming the place, speaking Spanish, carrying more things outside. *Drogas, drogas,* they kept saying, and the guilt was eating away at me.

"Jordan," Keira whispered, stepping out of the kitchen and coming over to me.

We stood there awkwardly standing in front of each other, me with my head down staring at her bare feet, her breathing heavily above me. Then she said, "We should go to my room."

I followed her up to her room and sat down on her bed. There were clothes on the floor and the closets and drawers were open.

"I see you're leaving."

"Yeah."

"To rehab."

She took a deep breath and sat down next to me. I looked at her hands; they were shaking.

Withdrawal, I thought. *Or maybe just fear.*

"Are you scared?" I asked her.

"No. Just…don't know what to expect. I guess, um, it's like going to a new school except worse." She put one of her hands over her eyes. "God, I already feel like crap and it's only been eight hours."

"I'm sorry." Tears were coming to my eyes. "I'm sorry for not doing anything."

"Oh, Jordan." She hugged me. "What could you have done?"

I pressed my face into her sweet-smelling blouse. "Something. Anything."

She squeezed me tighter. "I'm going to miss you so bad."

I rubbed my eyes and nodded into her shoulder and tried not to cry. And when her father called her to come downstairs because it was time for them to go and we all stood outside as the car moved out of the driveway and she opened the window to look back at me, all I could say to her was, "Be well," across the distance between us.

APRIL

I am lying on my bed and my mother comes in and tells me to vacuum the carpet because she and my father are going to pick my aunt and uncle up from the airport in Philadelphia. They will be staying over, which means the carpet cannot be dirty. My mother says, "Do you think you can handle it?" And I take the vacuum and plug it in, *whir-whir,* please let me ignore the sound of her voice. Please let me ignore their eyes, like, *poor Jordan, look at him, is he going to explode is he going to have a nervous breakdown what's happened to him my god my god.*

They go out of the house. I turn on the TV even though I can't even hear it over the noise of the vacuum cleaner. Doing nothing, just this mindless action of back and forth, feels so good. Completes my life. Except now my phone is vibrating.

"Jordan, hey, it's me. Hope you don't mind." Elizabeth is breathless for some reason. "What are you doing?"

"Cleaning the house and taking down the Christmas lights."

She says, "Your Christmas lights are still up?"

Before I can say yeah, she says, "You want me to help you take them down?"

"It's okay, I think I can manage."

"No, seriously. I'm a master at that kind of thing. Taking down Christmas lights. Even though I'm Jewish."

I laugh. "Then come over."

Elizabeth arrives half an hour after we hang up, earrings glittering and curls bouncing. We do some more mindless action in the living room and in the dining room, until finally I remember that my room is a frigging pigsty.

"Whoa," she says. "Um, no offense, but...your room is—"

"A shithole?" I suggest.

"Right."

We start with the clothes all over the floor. Every time she picks up a shirt or a pair of jeans, she asks me if it's clean or not. Everything is dirty or everything is of unknown status; she ends up putting it all in a laundry bag.

"I'm really organized," she explains.

"Then we're like opposites, 'cause I'm compulsively untidy."

"Your clothes are nice, though."

"They're okay. I just know how to match colors up, that's all."

Elizabeth picks up my pillow and sweeps some Fruit Roll-Up wrappers off the bed with her hands. That's when she sees the sweatshirt. It's half-hidden under the mattress, wrinkled and thick and covered in lint. She starts taking it by the hood and pulling it up, and I feel like I should protest or stop her or do something, at least, but I guess I'm tired. I stand there and watch her hold it up and sniff it to smell if it's dirty.

"Hey," she says finally, "is this clean?"

It isn't. "Yeah."

"Are you sure? It smells like Fruit Roll-Ups and old socks."

"It smells like old socks?" I snatch it from her and lift it to my nose. Old socks, sugar, deodorant...

"What's the matter?"

I hug the sweatshirt and press my face into the hood. Old socks, sugar, deodorant. Me. Her. *Gone.*

"Jordan." Elizabeth is in front of me, holding onto the sweatshirt, staring at me with her deep amber eyes. "It's hers, isn't it?"

"Her smell's gone. It doesn't smell like her anymore. I kept it because..."

"Because of the smell," she says. "I get it."

I take the sweatshirt and ball it up and drop it on the floor.

"What are you doing?"

"I need to throw it away."

She stares at me, her eyes wide. "Why?"

"It's useless."

She picks it up and folds it.

"Plus, we're done."

Elizabeth puts the sweatshirt down on my dresser and scoops up the wrappers on the floor. "We're done here, too. Um, I mean the room's fine now."

I don't need Keira's scent to sleep. I don't need Keira's scent to sleep. I don't need Keira to help me fall asleep. No, I don't. Yes? No.

"Okay," I say softly. "What do you want to do?"

"The lights?"

"Oh yeah. The lights."

We go outside and she helps me drag the ladder out of the shed. Once we've both gotten onto the roof, I suggest we start gathering the stuff up and putting it in a pile near the ladder so that one of us can throw the lights down and the other can put them away.

We work in silence for a few minutes until she says, "Is that Nat Starkley?"

I look up. "Where?"

She points to the street. I scoot closer to the edge of the roof to see. Sure enough, there's Nat in his stupid Subaru making out with stupid Sherry from AP Physics in the front seat of his car. He raises his head, his eyes sweeping over the house, finally settling on me. Sherry is still sucking his face, but he won't stop looking at me.

"He's still driving," Elizabeth says. "He could get into an accident."

Do you remember that time I held you when you thought your mom was going to die? Do you remember when you wet the bed at Blake Stewart's sleepover party in seventh grade and I told everyone it was me?

"Whatever," I say.

Nat's gaze is like, indestructible.

"But he's your best friend."

I tear my eyes away finally, just as he starts to open his mouth. I wait for the sound of the car speeding away, and then I say, "He used to be."

"What happened?"

"I became a mentally unstable, over-medicated piece of shit."

Her laughter surprises me. I turn to her and say, "What?"

"Did you make that up?"

"No, it's true. Ask anyone, they'll say the same thing just with different words. I am a slutty, depressing asshole."

She starts laughing again and then I start laughing even though I don't know why, and then I almost fall over the edge of the roof. Elizabeth has to pull me back.

"Damn," she says. "I didn't know you could be this happy. Are you taking like, Prozac or something?"

"Uh, well, it's all given to me, but I don't like it, so I don't take it."

She gets onto her knees and moves some of the lights into the pile near the ladder. "If you took it, do you think you'd feel better?"

I start climbing down. "No."

When I get to the bottom, she sticks her head over the side, throws down the lights, and starts coming down too. She lands on the ground and starts to say something else, maybe another question about my mental health, but I say, "Let's go inside and get something to eat."

We go into the kitchen and she sits down and looks at the pictures on the refrigerator. "You look like your brother."

"I look like my mom." I open the fridge and get out the bread and some strawberries. "You want French toast?"

"Sure."

I put a pan on the stove and turn it on. From the island Elizabeth says, "Um, aren't you going to put oil in that?"

"Oh yeah, on the bread, right?"

She giggles. "No, in the pan. Here, let me help."

She pours the oil into the pan, gets out a bowl, and cracks some eggs. "Pass me the cinnamon and sugar."

I give both jars to her and stand against the counter. "What else should I do?"

"You want to cut up some strawberries?"

"Yeah, I'll do that."

I slice the strawberries at the island and listen to her talk. She has an older sister named Hanna, and Hanna and their mom used to cook together in the kitchen and she'd sit at the table and draw and watch them, that's how she knows how to make food and stuff. She says I look like the kind of person who doesn't know how to cook. I laugh at that. She says, "Don't eat all the strawberries, Jordan," and I say, "Oh, was I eating them?" and she starts talking about how she goes to her aunt's house in the Hamptons, where the yard is full of strawberry plants. It reminds me of the weeks I used to spend on Martha's Vineyard. Seafood and shaved ice. My grandma slaved over that ajvar.

"You should come sometime," she says, sprinkling sugar over a slice of French toast. "We go a lot in the summer. You should come to my house, too."

"I should, shouldn't I? Where do you live?"

"Bay Shore."

"That's not so far. I'll stop by this week."

Her face lights up. "You don't have anything better to do?"

I elbow her and take a piece of French toast off the plate with two fingers. "Why, you want me to come in June?"

"Yeah, for my birthday." She watches me take a bite. "Is it good?"

"Yeah. Best French toast in the universe." I get a plate out from the cabinet and go to the fridge to get the maple syrup. "Elizabeth, you're an artist. What were you saying about your birthday?"

"Oh, I mean, if I have a birthday party. I might not have one, though. I haven't had one since elementary school."

"It's okay. I didn't have a party, either."

"When was your birthday?"

I take another bite of the French toast. "January."

"January? Crap, I knew you then. January what?"

"Um, the first."

She drops the spatula. "New Year's *Day*?"

"Mm-hmm." My mouth is full.

"So you're a New Year's baby."

"Ha ha, yeah. People are always surprised when they find out. I'm always the oldest. I'm older than you."

"Five months," she says. "That's nothing."

"Yeah, you're right." I move my plate so she can sit down next to me. "What day's yours? June what?"

"June fifth."

"Okay, right now I'm making a promise to myself that I will be at your house at midnight on June fifth to wish you happy birthday."

"Right now I'm making a promise to myself to be awake at midnight on June fifth when you come to wish me happy birthday."

"Swear over the beautiful, perfect French toast."

She shakes her head, smiling. "I swear."

Then we start talking about school and colleges, and we eat all the French toast, and after that my parents come home and we play games with Aida. I tell her she needs to meet Reed and Erin. She tells me I need to come to her house this week.

"I promise I'll come," I say, as she's leaving later on that evening.

She holds out her hand for me to shake. I take it and look up at her.

"I'm so happy I met you," she tells me. "I mean, I was so lonely here."

Her hand is soft and warm. Under the orange streetlights, her curly hair looks golden.

"Bye, Elizabeth," I say. I stand in the doorway to watch the car back out of the driveway and move onto the road.

"Jordan, come inside," my dad calls. "It's cold out there."

My mom says, "Come take your medication and go to bed."

"I'm coming," I answer, stepping back into the house behind the screen door.

It isn't cold. If it is, then I'm warm inside.

Elizabeth, I guess, I think suddenly, and then, *What the hell, maybe I'm just happy.*

Happy. It's really weird. I think that maybe I'd forgotten how warm you get sometimes.

pages taken from Keira de Luna's 12th grade diary, date unknown

This is a day with Robin.

When the morning comes, my mind goes, Fuck, the struggle begins, and like a gut reflex, because it's either I scratch my eyes out or I scour the bathroom for painkillers, I pick up the phone and call my sponsor. Robin. She's like thirty. She's got a lawyer husband and two daughters. She says they are the result of thirteen-year sobriety, and she's like, *imagine yourself like this*, and I try to imagine but that life is too far away from me right now.

Robin picks up fast and is like, "Morning, sunshine. Keira, what's up?"

"Nothing, really. Just woke up."

"Anything wrong?"

"I can't do this."

"What do you mean? Why?"

"I don't know, I just can't."

"How do you feel?"

I kind of pause, listening for movements in the house. Silence. Me and them.

"Bad," I say. "Unbelievably bad."

"Tell you what," Robin goes, "how 'bout you meet me at my place in an hour?"

Uh, no, fuck no. I do not want to go out into the light. I want to be Count Really-Effing-Blitzed, the reclusive dying vampire.

But anyway I'm like, "Sounds like a plan."

And when I hang up the phone, I start wishing I could go back to sleep and forget to wake up.

More silence until I hear mom's footsteps. She doesn't barge in; she's never done that, she gets scared too easily and she cares a lot about privacy and she is just too goddamn sweet. She knocks lightly and calls in her soft voice, "Keira, lovey, come eat some breakfast."

Usually she says, "Do you want breakfast?" to which I respond, "No," and she laughs and says, "Teenagers," and goes away. There is no choice here. I hear her breathing on the other side of the door. I go down in my pajamas.

The surface of the table is hardly fascinating, but I pretend to be interested in it anyway. Shiny shiny wood. Must be some kind of wax. Gloss. Dad is refusing to look at me because I've failed him, his daughter is a drug addict with raccoon eyes and unwashed hair, he keeps saying, "You are ruining your *own* life."

As a better form of distraction, I search my pants for my cell phone to text Jordan, ask if he wants to come over and eat breakfast with me to make things less awkward, but yes, I remember, he's in school. Duh. What the hell is he doing, anyway? Probably slumped over a desk in the front row, doodling in the margins of a notebook like he usually does. Prisms this time, or maybe Chinese dragons.

After a few minutes of aimless searching, I realize I don't even have any pockets.

Mom sets a steaming plate in front of me: eggs, toast, tomatoes, sausages, and tea. Shit on tea. Shit on eggs. Shit on all the un-sustaining sustenance in the universe.

"Maybe you can go for a long walk with Robin today," mom says cheerfully. "The weather is so nice."

Dad grunts. I say nothing. I hope he takes my eggs.

"Keira, eat something," she says.

I pick up the fork. Mom gets up and puts a bowl of cereal next to the plate. Fruit Loops. God. How in hell am I going to eat all this food? At the hospital, I wasn't even able to eat full meals till the second month, but at least I could eat snacks and little things before then. I can't eat at all anymore. The real world makes me want to throw up. That was how I spent the night after Jordan left, trying not to puke in his presence. He said, "Crap, I've got school tomorrow," and moved away from me. He forgot to kiss me goodbye. I wonder if he knows it made me sad. Obviously I wouldn't tell him.

"Keira," dad says. "Eat."

Okay, now I've got to remind myself to breathe. Don't think about the pills. When I leave the kitchen, I will take a shower and get dressed and not search the bedroom for any leftover drugs. I will finish my breakfast. I will not think about the pills. I will *not*.

Even though they fill you.

Robin's house is small and white, two towns over. The lawn is littered with children's toys and tricycles, I have to step over crap upon crap upon crap until I finally get to the flipping door. She comes out smiling and gestures for me to come out of the car. I bring my coffee with me so that one of my hands will have something to do while the other hides inside of my vest pocket. It's cheap gas station stuff, not my usual [Starbucks] because a) uh, I'm so broke, and b) don't I want to start a new life?—here, I imagine, a normal person would burst into song; a *High School Musical* number complete with full-on dancing in stairwells and singing into my fist, if only.

"Hey, kiddo," Robin goes, clapping me on the back, making me jump. "How's your morning been?"

"Uh, I actually don't remember."

She laughs. I wonder how a person can be so cheery. Why can't I be cheery like her? Why can't I be her kid— why can't she just *adopt* me? I'll clean her fucking lawn.

"I see you're dressed warm."

"Mm-hmm," or something like that, I murmur.

"Good. We're going to the lake."

My eyes feel like they're going to fall out of their sockets. The lake. I was like ten when I went there last. "To do what?"

"You ever gone boating, Keira?"

"No."

"Awesome. Then I'll get to show you something new." She grabs me by the arm. "We're taking my car."

Robin, in all honesty, makes me feel very antsy. I fidget in the car sitting next to her. The radio is on low; I wish it was blasting. I try to force myself to not think. *If I only had something to kill the pain,* I'm thinking.

"Falling asleep there, Keira?"

"Ha ha. No."

"We're almost there."

But shit, I think I'm going to throw up. I cover my mouth with my hand and roll down the window. Icy wind slaps at my face and slices into my eyes. Breathe. My nose tingles. It misses the powder. Breathe. Maybe, at home, I can pick the lock on the medicine cabinet and try to find something that will—

"You okay, honey? We're here."

A success story, yet again.

I follow her out of the car to the dock, where she pays to rent a boat that looks like one of those plastic things kids play with in the bathtub. Robin lets me sit first.

"All you have to do is pedal," she says. "See those things over there? Put your feet on them and pedal. I'll steer for us."

I do what she says and pedal, copying her motions. The boat moves slowly across the water. I look down and watch the bugs skate across the top. Robin asks me dumbass questions, What happened yesterday? How are your parents? Did you sleep well? Did you eat?

She tells me about her first day out of rehab a million years ago, and truthfully I just want her to shut up. Okay, I am *not* like her. She was addicted to meth and heroin. I only take prescription pills, that's nowhere near as bad as the shit she was doing. I'm better than her. *You're better, so much better, so now—*

She asks, "When are you going back to school?"

Ha-ha. Kidding me, right? School. I'm ruined there. Everyone knows what I did. Everyone talks about me. Returning to that place, I don't even want to think about it. It gives me cardiac arrhythmia.

And then my heart starts racing, and then I'm leaning over the edge of the boat and puking nastiness, colors I will not describe here, and it just keeps fucking going and going like some kind of demented machine. Then I feel Robin's hand on my back, hear her voice somewhere behind me, and then I'm wiping my leaky eyes and apologizing to her as she hands me tissues.

"It's okay, sweetie," she tells me softly. "It's okay. It's hard, I know."

"I can't do this, Robin."

"You can," she says. "You can conquer addiction."

"I'm not sick. Everyone at the rehab place and at the meetings tries to make it look like we all have a complicated disease, but we're not sick. There's a...there's a fucking difference."

"What's that difference?"

"The difference is that I'm doing this to myself, and those other people don't have a choice."

"So you have a choice?"

My hands are shaking. I start ripping the tissues to distract my fingers, something I've done since I was a kid. "Yes."

And Robin is like, predictably, "Then choose change. Choose change."

Bitch. As if it's that easy. Yes, tonight I will *change* my underwear, and tomorrow I will *change* my T-shirt. Bitch. I have chosen change.

We drive back to the house together so I can get my car and go home. Before I leave, I thank her (she did pay out of pocket for the boat and everything). She smiles and says, "Call me again tomorrow, promise?"

I promise.

Mom is still home. She meets me at the door and hugs me hard. She is so small, and it's weird because I don't remember her ever being this tiny, I only remember when she used to be big and strong. I remember when I used to fit in her arms. Her scent is comforting. I pull away and take off my jacket. Her eyes are wide and blue, ringed with dark purplish shadows; I don't want to see that so I look at my pictures. In the photos on the wall, I am sixteen, fourteen, eleven, eight, five, two, and just born. She was so happy. She doesn't sleep anymore. I've done that to her. I am a dick.

"Mommy," I say.

She looks up at me and her eyes are huge and blue like washing machines. I'm moving around in them but I'm still as dirty as I was three months ago.

I'm sorry. I'm sorry. A thousand times, I'm sorry.

"I'm just going to go take a nap."

She says okay in a shaky voice. In a shaky voice, she says she's going to go make lunch. Before I go, I kiss her cheek.

Upstairs under the covers. I'm not asleep, I'm having a conversation with the sky, skipping down the sidewalk with this feeling of being *loved* and *special* and *born to meet me and you and him and us* like everyone says. Reach up to the lights, it's The Height. And then I'm found.

But it's not real, it's just one of those dreams.

I sit at my desk, sliding my finger underneath a paperweight, examining it for any leftover powder. Gone, all gone. Someone must have cleaned.

I guess I'm relieved. I guess I'm disappointed. I get up and go into my parents' bathroom with one of Jordan's guitar picks, hoping that'll work. It's a Visa gift card, 'cause I bought him this thing that punches out guitar picks from any kind of material. It looks like a stapler. This is how, later, I will tell him I lost the gift card pick; flushed it down the toilet to stop myself from breaking into the medicine cabinet.

He will nod and say he understands, even though he doesn't. Not then.

Maybe never.

October 8, 2012

What happened after the awards ceremony: nothing.

I didn't go to school. I didn't go to the funeral. Two weeks in my room, dead, wishing I was dead, dying from the nightmares. *I saw her gone.* She was blue and not breathing and I couldn't kiss her to life. I couldn't bring it all back to her. There were holes in me. My mother came to hold me and shed these random tears, maybe a thousand times, and I looked up at her and said, "Why are *you* crying, Mom?"

Three weeks. The de Lunas wanted to take me to court, and my sister told me that wouldn't happen, it was just something people said when they were really upset over wrongful death. Wrongful death, because it was wrongful, because I was there—I saw her gone. Her mother's nails in my right eye, the surgeons said the damage was permanent. My mother cried when she changed the bandages. I said, "Why are you *crying*, Mom? *Why*?"

Three weeks and many days. I kept screaming, "Fuck you," it was the only thing I could think of to make them go away, then they'd go away, then I'd cry. I was always crying. Even before all of this.

A long time after. My dad unlocked the door with a key, stood over my face, and said, "Get up right now. You're late. I'm driving you."

He was using *that voice*. I'm-pissed-as-hell-this-morning-so-don't-try-anything-with-me-today-don't-look-at-me-don't-speak. I dragged myself out of bed and showered and threw on some clothes. Everything smelled like her bed sheets. I dumped the suit I'd worn on Saturday in a trash bag, tied it up, and put on a sterile eye patch.

The ride to school seemed shorter than it usually was. I sat in the backseat and stared out the window. Everything looked different; more vast and unfamiliar. The school was like another planet. I stumbled out of the car and heard my dad ask if I wanted him to walk me in.

"No," I replied; I wondered why he'd even bothered.

The hallways were empty because everyone else was in class. I got a late pass from the office and wasted time standing at my locker organizing notebooks by color. Freaking ROYGBIV.

"You know, fuck it," I muttered, shutting the door. I needed to get it all over with. Slide into a seat next to my friends and explain everything. *Explain what?*

I told myself to shut up. I picked up my backpack and walked to my math class.

"Sorry I'm late," I told the teacher, handing her the late pass.

"No worries, Jordan. Just get the notes from someone."

"Okay."

Everyone was staring at me. I sat down in my usual seat next to Audra and started opening my binder, blinded by humiliation.

"Hey," Audra hissed. "Hey, where the fuck have you been, asshole?"

"Sorry."

"Is it true what everyone's been saying?"

"What's everyone been saying?"

"Jordan," the teacher said. "You're already late. What gives you the right to interrupt my class with your irrelevant conversation?"

"Sorry," I said for the third time, looking down at the string of numbers in my math textbook so I didn't have to meet all those eyes.

The classroom went quiet. The numbers became shapes and letters and squiggly lines. Audra passed me her notes and pointed to the bottom of the first page: *u dont know what ppl have been saying??*

I turned around and shook my head at her. The teacher said, "Jordan, turn around and pay attention."

I turned back to the papers on my desk, and for the rest of the period, I copied the notes. The numbers became snakes. Everyone was a snake.

Fifth period gym class, I finally found out what was going on. Nat, Alec, Josh, and Audra caught me at the doors asking me a hundred questions at once, and I had to shout, "I don't know what you're talking about, so someone explain everything to me," three times before they all calmed down.

"What are people saying?" I asked them.

"The whole school's talking about how the de Lunas want to press charges against," Alec said. "Because she's dead, because of you."

The de Lunas. Her mom and dad. I'd forgotten they existed. Had I really forgotten they existed?

"What?"

"Jordan," he said. "Because…Jordan, you just left the ceremony, and after her parents found her, I don't know, maybe they told the police you were there, and the police kept calling people and asking them where you were, and Elisa said, uh…"

"Said what? Just tell me."

"She said she met you at the train station," Audra said. "She said you were like, having a mental breakdown and going on about how you let Keira die because you were too tired or something and you didn't know what to do and you were going to get arrested."

"Did you really do that?" Josh looked at me. "I mean, did you sit there and watch her and think that maybe she'd be better off dead anyway?"

"Josh," Nat said.

"Shut up, Nat, that's what everyone's saying."

"Nat," I said. "Who told you guys?"

"So it's all true?"

"Who told you all this stuff?"

"Elisa," Alec said. "Elisa told me."

"What class does she have this period?"

"You're such a douche bag," Audra said to me. "You're going to go blame Elisa when you were the one who got yourself into the mess you're in?"

"Shut up, Audra!"

"Everyone told you to stay away from that girl! You're an idiot, Jordan! You *are*!"

"Go fuck yourself, Audra! You don't know shit!"

"How could I, when you cursed me to hell and back every time I came to your house to see you? I don't know shit, so fucking tell us what really happened!"

"*Nothing* really happened, that's the problem, you bitch!"

They started calling after me but I was already gone, running down the hall away from the gym and all the people who didn't know if they should trust me anymore.

It was raining outside. I stood under the tarp at the side door and scrolled through my contacts. Elisa's number was one of the firsts among the *E*'s. I texted her: *where r u*

Seconds later she texted me back: *free pd*

come to the side door. im waiting.

It took her around fifteen minutes to get there. She was wearing a waterproof jacket and flower-printed rain boots. In the dim light, she looked absolutely beautiful.

"Jordan," she said. "Are you mad at me?"

I unwrapped a piece of gum and put it in my mouth. I gave her a stick, too. A peace offering, sort of. "No."

"Jordan, I was only telling the truth. People kept asking me what had happened when you left the ceremony. What was I supposed to say?"

"I don't know, Elisa. Maybe nothing?"

"I didn't think it would get out of control like this, people making up all these shitty rumors about murder and crap. You shouldn't have even gone over to see her. I told you to stay with us. You said no."

"She was in trouble, Elisa!"

"Well, what was I supposed to do, Jordan? Lie for no reason? There wasn't even anything wrong with what I told them! All I said was that you went to see Keira and the next morning you were so messed up you could barely speak in full sentences! Is that so wrong?"

I blew a bubble and sat down on the steps. She sat next to me. She asked me if I was okay, and all of a sudden I didn't give a damn about anything anymore.

"I'm fine," I told her. "I'll be fine."

There were tears sparkling in her eyes. "I told you to stay with us. I told you to stay but you wouldn't listen."

"It's okay, Elisa."

"I'm not the one who said you let her die. I would never say something like that about you." The tears in her eyes were coming down her face. "I swear, I never said that."

"It's okay, it's okay. I don't care." I spit the gum out into the grass. "The bell's ringing. You should go."

She took both of my hands and looked at me. "What about the de Lunas? What are you going to do?"

I shook my head. "Forget about that. Go. You're going to be late."

Elisa was crying. She pulled open the door and went into the building. I turned around and walked down the steps. The rain was still falling pretty hard, but all I had to do was walk down the road to the plaza, where I could catch a bus.

The rumors, they were all okay. It didn't matter. I mean, nothing really mattered to me.

Nothing else really happened that day after I left the school. I took the bus to the library and spent hours in the children's section curled up on the bean bag chairs, watching Netflix on my phone until my eyes couldn't take it anymore.

AUGUST 3, 2012

It was the summer before Keira went off to college and her parents had invited me to their house on Fire Island. My parents didn't want to let me go, but since I was extremely psyched about it and wouldn't take no for an answer, they gave their okay (provided that there would be adult supervision at all times). The day we were set to leave, my mom held me for a long time and tried to come up with excuses to make me stay.

"You don't want to spend time with your brother before he goes to Duke in August?" she asked me.

I looked at Francis, who was looking away. "I've been spending time with him, haven't I?"

To my surprise, my mom actually laughed.

"All right, fine," she said. "Go have fun."

My dad said, "Don't get into any trouble."

"I won't."

More hugs, and then I was on a ferry with Keira and her parents and her cousin Ashlee, who was from Scotland and had an accent. She was eighteen and really pretty too, with very pale skin and golden freckles and green eyes. She laughed a lot and used funny slang.

We spent the nights camping out on the beach behind the house and exploring the place during the day. It was nice going into town, the three of us holding hands, Keira in the middle and Ashlee and me on the other sides. Keira knew a ton of the old people around, so she'd always wave and say hi and then introduce us.

We also spent a lot of time at the neighbors' house, where Keira's childhood friend Katya and her brother Liam lived. Liam was eighteen like Ashlee and Keira, and Katya was nineteen. So technically, for most of the time, it was the five of us hanging out.

This one night, we sat on Liam and Katya's deck huddled under a bunch of blankets, me leaning against Keira with my guitar in my arms and Liam flirting with Ashlee while she and Katya sang along to whatever I started playing. It was kind of cold out (hence the blankets), and the air was full of ocean and fireflies. I said that out loud. Keira laughed.

"The air," she said sarcastically, "is full of love."

"No duh," said Katya. "Look, your parents' bedroom light is still on."

"That doesn't mean anything. The last time my parents even kissed was ten years ago, on their anniversary. And I made them do it."

"Funny," I said, strumming a D minor chord, "I thought your parents loved each other."

"They do. Just not the way normal people do."

"And how do normal people love each other?" Ashlee giggled, taking the scotch from Liam.

When she said that, Keira's mood changed suddenly. She pushed me away and got up.

"Where're you going?" Katya asked.

"The bathroom."

When she had disappeared through the glass doors into the house, Liam took the bottle from Ashlee and looked at me and said, "God, she's so hot. You're lucky, Jordan."

"Thanks." I was distracted, watching the doors, wondering if it was me.

"How was it, anyway?" Liam asked. "I mean, dealing with all of it."

"What?"

"Like, you know. She was on drugs."

"Well, I don't know. I tried. I did…whatever. She's better now. It's just college that her mom's scared of, 'cause of peer pressure and shit."

"Yeah, that's another thing."

"Yeah."

"She'll be okay, though."

"Yeah."

Keira came back and sat down next to me. I held my breath. Was it me? Was it something I'd done?

And then she took my hand underneath the blanket, and everything was fine again. I started playing Lynyrd Skynyrd. She said, "I think they're showing an outdoor movie at the park."

"You saw that from the bathroom window?" Liam asked, and Ashlee and Katya started laughing.

"Yeah, dude, night vision." Keira smiled. "We should go."

"Now? Man, it's like eleven."

"It's *Titanic*. C'mon, we have to go."

"I've seen that a million times," Katya said.

"Same."

Then Liam was like, "Well anyway, let's just fucking go. I mean, there's nothing to do. Let's just go."

We gathered up the blankets and rode the bikes there. Katya sat on my handlebars and pretended to be my eyes, and we almost fell over six times. Liam said, "You look like a douche, Jordan," and I wanted to say something about that but I was out of breath from pedaling and laughing.

The park was mostly full of kids our age sitting around and drinking. We set ourselves up in the back and sprawled out on top of the blankets. The movie was still at the beginning. Katya and Ashlee started drooling over

Leonardo DiCaprio's face and the rest of us lay there in silence. I was bored and kind of sleepy but forcing myself to stay awake because it would have been lame to fall asleep like that. There was a salty breeze coming off the ocean towards us, making the grass move back and forth. Stupid movie, Jack dying for no reason because of stupid-ass Rose. Why didn't she fucking trade places? Why didn't she ever fucking *think* about *him*?

Keira's hand was on my shoulder.

"Let's go somewhere," she said. The same way she always said it outside of the school or on the phone or in a text, taking my breath away.

"Where?"

"Ice cream."

I got up and followed her even though I knew there weren't any ice cream shops open at this time of night. She was walking fast; I had to speed up to get closer to her. I tried to catch her eyes, but she wouldn't look my way.

"Slow down," I said. "Please."

She stopped unexpectedly and stretched her arms out, looking up at the sky. "Jordan, I've been using."

My legs went weak. "Yeah?"

She said, "It was more than Percocet."

Always, always, forever and ever and ever. My vision was blurring. My mind was on repeat. Always this. Again and again. She touched me and I couldn't breathe.

She was saying, *"I'm sorry."*

She was saying, *"I think we should break up. For both of us, but you especially. I know you don't understand."*

She was saying, *"I love you."*

"Why?" I asked, staring down at my bare feet. The grass hurt. The air going in and out of my lungs hurt. Me trying to understand, that hurt most of all. "Why for *me?*"

"It's too much for you, baby."

"*I* decide what's too much for me. Not you."

She sighed, and her breath came out all minty over my face. She bent over and kissed my forehead. She said, "It's not a choice, Jordan."

We went back to the movie—separately, not together. I got there before her, just in time to see that Liam and Ashlee were hooking up under my quilt. Katya called my name and asked me where I'd been. I didn't answer.

"What's wrong?" she said. "You want to sleep? Come here. Come over here, sweetie."

I scooted closer to her and she put her blanket over me and held me. She smelled like scotch and some expensive perfume. Keira returned and sat down next to Ashlee and Liam. I felt Keira breathing, like her lungs were underground and the earth was shaking and the vibrations were going through me. I wanted to cry but instead I closed my eyes and tried to pretend I couldn't feel her at all.

It was really early when I woke up, and at first I didn't know where I was, but then I remembered the outdoor movie. And then I remembered everything else.

I pushed Katya off me and put the blanket over her. She rolled over a little, but she didn't open her eyes. Next to Ashlee, Keira was asleep with her head in the grass. I closed my eyes for a few minutes. Then I opened them, stepped over her legs, and picked up my flip-flops. We were done. *We were actually done.*

I rode my bike back to the house, trying to get myself to stop thinking. I pictured myself as a little kid, riding my bike through Central Park with Erin and Francis and my dad and Aida in a baby seat behind him. I thought about the smells of New York City in the late afternoon and the feeling I got in my stomach when my dad used to pick me up and hold me high above his head, then bring me down and tickle my sides. My mom singing "Hey Jude" in the night while Francis, Erin, and I lay side by side in Erin's pink princess bed, pretending to be asleep. Keira singing "Hey Jude" with the Beatles on the radio.

I threw my bike against the steps and went around to the back door. The house was quiet and dark as hell.

"Jordan?" Keira's dad said, coming out of the kitchen. "Where's Keira? Where is Ashlee?"

"They're, uh. They're back at the park, they're still asleep."

"Oh, well, they'll come later, right?" He gave me a weary smile. "I was just making some coffee. Do you want breakfast?"

"Um, no." I started biting my thumbnail, which was something I hadn't done in about seven years. "I actually have to go. My, uh, mom called. My aunt, she…she…had a pet shark, and like, it like ate her in the bathtub."

What the hell, he seemed to believe it. And if he didn't, then at least he pretended to. "Oh my God. I'm sorry."

He wanted to say some more sympathetic shit, but I couldn't take it. "It's okay, it's okay, I never knew her. She doesn't live here, she lives in, like, Malaysia. My parents keep calling and calling me, though, so I have to go. I'm going to get my stuff."

He followed me upstairs and watched me pack up my things. "I'm so sorry about your aunt, Jordan. Please send our condolences."

"I will."

"It would have been nice if you had stayed longer."

I felt my eyes burn. "I know."

"I can drive you back home. Let me get dressed."

"No, no, it's fine. My parents are already waiting at the…um, the place. All I have to do is take the ferry. I can do it myself, it's fine."

"Are you sure?"

"Yes, absolutely."

But I ended up leaving the house after Mrs. de Luna fried me some pancakes and made me a lunch to take on the ferry. When I finally finished breakfast and announced, for the fourth time, that I really needed to go, she hugged me for a long time, and I almost burst into tears when she did that. I don't know why. Those kinds of emotions just come to me out of nowhere sometimes. She asked me if I'd said goodbye to Keira already, and I said yes and felt really fucking bad about it.

"She's going to miss you a lot when she goes to college in the fall," she said. "She told me."

"Yeah," I agreed softly. "Yeah, same. Uh, can you tell her I love her and hope she makes good decisions…and that I'm proud of her because she told me the truth?"

"What truth?" Mrs. de Luna asked.

I smiled at her and it was painful. "It's nothing. Something between the two of us. Thank you for letting me spend part of the summer with you guys. I had a great time."

They wanted me to at least wait until Keira and the others woke up so that Liam and Katya's parents could also say goodbye to me, but I told them I couldn't. Mr. de Luna drove me to the dock and I got on the ferry. It was around nine o'clock and the sun was weak. Like me.

I sat down on a bench and fell asleep, and an old lady had to wake me up when we reached the Long Island shore. That was when I realized that I didn't even have a ride.

I didn't want to bother my parents because they'd ask me a ton of questions and probably call Mr. and Mrs. de Luna, so I called Erin. She didn't pick up. She's a super deep sleeper, especially over the breaks. I called Aida hoping she'd give the phone to Erin, but she didn't pick up either, which was a shock because she has ears like a bat, or whichever animal.

Shit, I thought, *now I have to call Francis.*

"Jor," he mumbled when he picked up, "hey. What is it?"

And just like that, hearing his voice, I started crying.

"Francis, can you come get me?"

"Hey," he said. "Hey, what is it? Where the hell are you?"

"Fire Island. The ferry. Please come, Francis, please come."

"I'm coming. Don't go anywhere. Don't cry. I'm coming, I promise."

I said okay, hung up, and sat down on the curb. Reality began rushing into me way too fast—I buried my head in my arms and cried and cried and cried. I cried for almost twenty minutes until the ferry supervisor or whoever came up to me and asked me if I was okay. So I dried my eyes and counted people: people going onto the ferry, people coming off the ferry, people walking around. I made up stories for them. I tried to guess their personalities by the way they smiled and laughed. The car came and there was Francis in the driver's seat, looking so un-Francis-like that I couldn't tell what he was feeling.

He got out and I stood up and we both looked at each other from that distance. Then he came closer and took my stuff.

"Go sit in the car," he said. "I'll put this in the back."

I sat down and wiped my runny nose with my hoodie sleeve. Francis shut the door to the backseat and slid in next to me, turning so that we were face to face.

"Jordan," he said. "What happened?"

I told him about all of it. The day before, the beginning of the year, my sixteenth birthday. Things from months ago and things from minutes ago. I told him about how much I loved Keira. And then I said, "But we're over."

There was a long silence. I realized the radio was not on. Francis never turns on the radio unless someone else does it for him.

"I'm going to be honest with you right now," he said finally. "I'm glad she broke up with you. And she's right for doing that."

I rubbed my nose with my sleeve again. "But I love her, Francis."

"I know you do, bro. I know. You'll be okay soon."

He leaned over and hugged me. Francis hugging me. That was another thing I needed to remember—Francis hugging me and telling me he understood, and that I didn't deserve to get hurt like this. Then I was crying again and he was apologizing for the things he thought he should've done.

He started driving a few minutes later, when we'd both calmed down enough to put on our seatbelts. He told me he was sorry. I shook my head and thanked him.

"For what?" he asked.

"Stuff," I said.

And I lay back with my head against the window and pretended to fall asleep so I wouldn't have to talk.

APRIL

When I wake up, I look at the ground before I look up at the ceiling. Elizabeth is sitting on the floor in front of my bed watching some morning talk show.

"Hey," she says as I push back the covers and reach for my glasses.

"Are you hungry? Did you eat?" I throw on an old Tokio Hotel T-shirt.

"Yeah, your mom gave me some cereal. She's really nice."

"Thanks." More like she's just ecstatic to see me hanging out with living, breathing people my own age. "Um, you want to go downstairs and wait for Reed and Joni?"

"Sure." She is blushing. "Sorry."

"For what?" I pretend to not know what she's talking about. I cross the room and open the door.

"Staring. You have a nice figure."

Ah, Elizabeth, so candid. "Lacrosse and taekwondo, that's why."

"You do taekwondo?"

"Used to. When I was younger."

Her eyes go big. "Oh my God, what belt are you?"

"I got up to brown and then I quit."

"Why?"

"I don't know, I ran out of time. Couldn't fit it into my schedule anymore."

We are standing in the kitchen now, and my dad and Aida are at the table eating breakfast.

"Hi, Elizabeth," Aida says. "Joni and Reed are here, Jordan."

"What? Where?"

"In the den with Mommy."

I grab a Pop Tart off her plate and leave the kitchen, Elizabeth trailing after me.

They're sitting on the couch, playing Minecraft and talking to my mom at the same time.

"Hi, guys," I yell, and they both jump on top of me like crazy people, yelling, "Jordan, Jordan, *Jordan!*"

When I'm finally able to push them off, I pull Elizabeth into the room and say, "Reed, Joni, this is Elizabeth. Elizabeth, this is Joni and Reed."

"Wait," Reed interrupts, "you're Elizabeth? *The* Elizabeth?"

Elizabeth starts blushing again. "Um, no…just Elizabeth…"

"No. You're *the* Elizabeth. Jordan's told me about you. From what I hear, you're like hashtag awesome, aren't you?"

"Um, I don't know."

"She is," I say. "She totally is."

"She's adorable, too." Joni makes eyes at me.

"Goddamnit, shut up." I grab their hands. "Are you guys hungry?"

They shake their heads.

"Well, I am. Let's go to the kitchen. I'll be fast, don't worry."

Joni leans in towards Elizabeth and whispers, "Jordan's not a morning person at all. He's like, completely irritable at this time of day."

Elizabeth laughs softly. "He's not that bad."

"Look, Jor," Reed says to me. "We'll buy something on the way, okay? The tour starts at eleven and we're not even in the car."

I look at my watch, and shit, it's nearly ten. We leave the house and get into my car. Loud, obnoxious pop jams make the car doors vibrate.

"Should you really be driving?" Reed asks me. "I mean, your eye. Like, aren't you having another surgery soon?"

"Yeah, whatever, that's in May. It's April. I'm fine."

"You sure?"

"Yeah. Stop talking about it."

Then Joni, my savior, changes the subject. "So, Elizabeth, did Jordan tell you who we are?"

"Um, his best friends from the beginning of time?"

"Reed and I are Joni's husbands," I explain quickly, with my mouth full of egg and bagel. "We all got married in third grade."

"Did you and Joni date?"

"No," Joni says. "That's why you shouldn't feel threatened. He has a nice mouth, just letting you know."

"Jeez, Joni, can't you figure out when to not talk?"

"Aw," says Reed. "Elizabeth's blushing again. Elizabeth's so cute. You should kiss Jordan right now, Elizabeth, and become his second wife."

"I, uh," Elizabeth says.

"You know what," I break in irritably, "just stop. Both of you. You're being over-the-top annoying."

"We didn't mean to do that, Elizabeth," Reed says. "We're just weird."

"It's okay!" Elizabeth is laughing. "You and Joni are really funny. I heard people from New York City were stuck up but I guess not all of them are."

"Do you have famous parents? California kids almost always have famous parents, right?"

She laughs again. "My parents are *not* famous."

Joni starts unwrapping one of the chocolate bars she made me buy her at the gas station. "Why did you move here?"

"Oh, because my sister goes to Stony Brook and she got sick last year. We came here to be close by, just in case and stuff."

"Wow," I say, because I hadn't known that. "I'm sorry."

"It's all right. She's all right."

I glance at her to see if she really means that, but instead of looking at her expression, I find myself realizing she has a bunch of blond hairs among the orange. With the light coming through the window, her irises look yellow. I almost tell her something stupid like *you have such beautiful eyes,* but I stop myself just in time. We spend two hours singing along to the crap on the radio, stopping for pee and snack breaks, and talking about school and TV shows like a bunch of bland, normal teenagers would.

Finally, finally, we enter Providence, arrive late, and wander around aimlessly for like an hour before we finally meet an admissions officer who directs us to the right group. The dude leading us around is a kid: twenty or twenty-one. I fight to get to the front of the pack with my notepad and pen, and constantly have to shush Reed and Joni, who're sniggering and make plans to roam around behind me. Elizabeth stays next to me, taking photos of the campus with her phone. When we bump into each other, she blushes and I feel my face burn.

Before the information session, when we're waiting for Elizabeth at the vending machines near the bathroom, Joni says, "Jordan, why don't you and Elizabeth go out?"

"Well, Joni, you first have to like somebody before you go out with them."

"But you like Elizabeth," she points out. "And she likes you."

I choke on a chip and start coughing. "How the fuck would *you* know if I liked Elizabeth?"

"The way you look at her. The way she looks at you."

"You should ask her to Junior Prom," Reed says. "Or whatever they have at your school."

"It's the Junior Social."

"Whatever. You should ask her."

"Why can't I just wait for her to actually tell me she likes me first?"

"Um, no offense Jordan, but no one sane is going to have the guts to ask out the psychotic school super-murderer."

"Thanks a million. Screw you."

"Dammit, you know what I mean. She's too shy. She's that type. Plus, she's new to your school and you're like, her only friend in the place. You should ask her."

"I'm not asking," I say, just as Elizabeth comes out of the bathroom.

We go to the information session and I sit there quietly, as if I'm actually listening to the admissions director, when really I'm busy thinking about Elizabeth. Wouldn't it be great to be in love with someone like her—predictable, sweet, ordinary?

The thoughts are still running through my head even after the session ends and we're leaving the campus to go to a nearby deli. We get our food and Elizabeth huddles next to me in the booth, playing thumb war across the table with Reed. I can't stop thinking about how cute she is. I also can't stop thinking about how I might not be ready for a relationship, especially since it hasn't even been that long, and she deserves to be with someone who is emotionally sound. Plus, I'm not even planning on going to the Junior Social, although I'd gone to prom last year when Keira took me. We only spent half an hour there before she asked me if I wanted to take a detour, and we got into the car and drove to the beach and played in the waves in the dark. She'd been so deliriously happy that night, talking to me about marriage and love and running away. Hydrocodone does that to you. I didn't think of it at the time.

But alas, my friends (former friends, actually) are all going to the Social. Audra's going with Mitch Qasim, this dude who plays first violin in orchestra and thinks I suck at cello. Nat's going with Sherry, of course, and Alec has Inna Newman, the student council secretary, and Josh already asked Zoey Osunde, the president of the African American Student Organization. Even my lax boys have dates, what the hell. And I plan to go home that day, buy three cartons of cookies and cream, and finish them all before the end of a ten-hour movie marathon alone in my room.

"I'm going to Junior Prom with Lisi Jerred," Reed is saying when I stop thinking about the Social. "You remember her, right Jordan?"

"Yeah," I say, even though I don't.

"Lisi's really hot," says Joni. "But she's not hotter than me. Only Nico is."

"Nico's a dickhead. You have absolutely no taste in the human race."

"Look at Nico." She holds up her phone. "Just look at him. Admire the heat."

"Elizabeth, let me show you the Cup Song."

I look up at the clock on the wall. Fuck, still can't read it. "Show it to her and then let's go. My mom says we have to be back before dinner."

Elizabeth's hands are sort of small and soft, not like Keira's slender piano fingers. She keeps getting confused about which hand does what. I wonder if she knows how to dance, and then remember she'd done ballet for years. There are framed studio photos of her in costumes on the walls at her house.

If I'd been there to see that bitch call her fat, I think to myself in the car behind the steering wheel, *I'd have...*

She is asleep against the window, snoring softly with her mouth open. The car is quiet except for the sounds of water droplets coming from the puzzle game Joni's playing on her phone. My head feels empty. Unconsciously, I think of Keira soaking wet in the moonlight.

Shit. I need to get myself together. I try to concentrate on the road and count each beige and silver car in sight, a therapeutic tactic that makes me feel normal even though doing it isn't.

It's nearly dark by the time we get back. I don't want to wake Elizabeth because she looks so happy sleeping against her seatbelt, but I can't leave her here either.

"Elizabeth," I whisper. "Liz. Wakey-wakey."

Her eyes open one at a time and she yawns. "Where are we?"

"New York," Reed says. "Boring Long Island."

Elizabeth's rubbing her eyes. "Oh, right."

The house smells of lasagna and baked vegetables. Out of nowhere, Erin appears at the door full of alma-mater spirit: Barnard sweatpants, Barnard sweatshirt and Columbia slippers.

"So this is Elizabeth," she says, grinning. "I've heard so much about you."

"I told you," Reed says. "*The* Elizabeth."

"Yeah, Jordan, what's that about?" Joni nudges me.

I swat her away. "She's great. Can we eat?"

And dinner is basically the same as the information session; mouths move and Erin talks about college and I zone out, locked into my worries about school and the Social. People ask me questions and I keep saying, "What?" and my mom says, "The medication makes him tired," which is embarrassing and not the case at all.

Elizabeth's mom arrives when we're watching *Fast Five* in my room after we've finished eating. She is in a deep conversation with my parents when we come down, the three of them laughing about shit they don't bother to tell us. I introduce her to Reed and Joni, and Reed says, "Can she come again tomorrow?"

"Do you want me to drop you off?" Mrs. Mischel asks Elizabeth.

"Yeah, we'll have tons of fun," I say. "We'll go to all the awesome places I can think of."

"Which are very limited here on Long Island," Reed points out. "Come to the city."

Elizabeth laughs. "No, it's okay. I have to write a paper. I guess I'll see you guys next time?"

"Definitely."

We go out onto the porch to wait while her mom finishes talking to my parents, although Reed and Joni have decided to stay inside with my sisters. It's a little chilly out. I can hear her yawning in the dark.

"Hey, Elizabeth," I say.

"What?"

"Do you, um, want to go to the Junior Social? With me?"

It takes her a while to answer. In the moment before she opens her mouth, I start worrying that maybe she doesn't like me after all, or maybe I've asked too early, or maybe she hadn't wanted to go to the Social in the first place. But then she says, "I'd love to go with you," and I exhale.

Reed and Joni burst through the door then, and Reed shouts, "I'm awesome! I knew it, I fucking *knew* it!"

"I'm so proud of you!" Joni shrieks, throwing her arms around my neck, and I think about the fact that they are such kids, Reed and Joni, partners in colorful, ridiculous crime.

A few seconds later, Mrs. Mischel comes out with my mom and they start walking to the car.

"I guess I'm going now," Elizabeth says, her voice light with emotion.

"Wait," Reed calls after her. "I just want to say thank you. I want to thank you for doing whatever it is you do."

"Whatever it is I do?"

"Jordan. He's so much better. You should've seen him before. He's so much better now. Because of you, I think. So thank you."

Reed, he's such a frigging nerd. I sit down on the steps and try not to cry. He catches up with Elizabeth, puts his hands on her shoulders, and hugs her hard.

"I love you, kid," he says. "I love you so much."

And then I actually do start crying, and Joni starts crying, and then we all start crying. Our moms look at us like we're crazy and ask us, from afar, if we're okay.

"Yeah," Joni tells them, wiping her eyes. "Yeah, we're good."

We're still teary when Elizabeth gets into the car and her mom starts driving, and we stand on the lawn trying to wave to her. We don't stop until my dad begins calling for us. Elizabeth doesn't stop until we've gone away. I know because I kept looking back.

ENTRY #16: LIFE

The last play we ever did was called "Angels! The Tragedy". I was nearly sixteen and a half then, still supportive, still hopeful. Kai wrote the script and got one of the chorus kids to help him with the music and composition. He said it only took him a month to complete.

"Angels! The Tragedy" was a Vietnam War story about these boys who get drafted into the army in 1968 even though none of them know anything about warfare, but then one of them falls in love with a Vietnamese village girl who claims she is anti-communist. Everyone sort of shuns him, especially his best friend Roman, with whom he made a pact to have each others' backs no matter what. Later on, communist Vietnamese guerilla fighters catch the boy with the village girl and both of them are killed, and Roman, who finds their bodies, shoots himself in the foot so that he can go back to the States with the boy's body to bury him.

Everyone thought it was all very depressing. Alec was like, "Do we really have to do a play about death for the spring show?"

"Death?" Kai said. "Who said this play's all about death?"

"Um, this thing is filled with dead people."

He shook his head. "You guys don't understand. The play is about *life*, not death. The fragility and sacredness of life. That's what it's about. It's not death. Read the script over again and you'll see."

I did, but I still didn't see.

We rehearsed at Kai's house because he didn't think the advisor would approve of all the fake blood and plastic guns that had to go into the entire performance. I was cast as Roman and this guy named Wade got the part of Thomas, the boy who's supposed to be Roman's best friend.

Wade, for some reason, hated me with a fiery passion. Rumor had it that he'd been in love with Keira and was jealous; rumor also had it that I'd forgotten to give him back a pen in seventh grade and that kind of thing was his number one pet peeve. Whatever the problem was, he never spoke to me unless he had to.

He talked to everyone else though, especially Sonja Hamish, the girl he had to kiss. She's Nepalese and probably one of the most gorgeous girls I've ever seen in my life. She was the Vietnamese village girl, and for most of the play she didn't speak. When she did, she only spoke some language that I didn't believe was Vietnamese even though Kai said it was. It sounded like a mix of Japanese and mispronounced Spanish.

Anyway, so Sonja's brother Rahul is my brother Francis's best friend, and for that reason we know each other pretty well, and she kept telling me she wished I'd gotten the part of Thomas instead of Roman.

"You're not a Roman," she said. "Roman is weak. You're strong, like Thomas."

"Roman isn't weak."

"Maybe, but you're not like him."

I shrugged and said yeah, but I really did love Roman. He isn't brave like Thomas, but he has a sort of bravery of his own; a kind of admirable loyalty. When Thomas dies, he stops being a boy and becomes a man.

"It's really important that you let the audience see that you've changed," Kai told me. "Body language, voice, expression. It's everything."

To do that, I had to transport myself to a Vietnamese jungle and become a wide-eyed kid soldier from the sixties. The hardest parts were the pain and the love. It was all in the eyes; I had to close them, lower my eyelids, force brimming tears, etc. I had to turn to the audience and show them my heart. I had to make them swim in my eyes.

The play had to be amazing not just because it was our last one with Kai, but because Keira was actually excited to see it; since she'd gotten out of rehab in late March, this was the first and last play she would ever see me perform. We were not really hanging out much in school because she didn't want her bad reputation to rub off on me in public, she said—even though I really didn't mind. I mean, I knew she was in pain. I didn't think she wanted me to talk about school. So most of the time when we hung out I didn't say anything at all, just listened to her talk and read poetry in her bedroom. Apparently she was irritated that I hadn't told her about the play.

"How come I had to find out from someone else?" she prodded. "How come you couldn't tell me yourself?"

"I don't know," I said. "I guess I just didn't think of it."

She pinched my cheek, pretending to be mad. "Look out for me, then, because I'm going to be there."

And sure enough, when the curtains opened and I'd taken my place at the fence in front of my fake house, hugging my fake mom and pretending to wipe away my fake tears, I looked out and saw her sitting there in the back row, holding up her phone to take pictures. My mind wanted to keep making me look out at the audience, keep thinking *Keira, Keira,* but I had to force it to focus on Roman. I had to be a nineteen-year old American soldier in Vietnam. *The Things They Carried* and *Fallen Angels.*

Thomas's dead body lying next to the village girl's, eyes open, plastic leaves falling.

"Shit," I whispered, completely unscripted, and my mic picked it up so that my own voice echoed around the room.

I was Roman. I knelt down and looked at him, into his blue eyes that had once held life. I took a deep breath and touched the bullet wound.

I know what this is about now, I realized, as I stood up and took the plastic gun out of my belt. I pointed it at my foot and pulled the trigger. The sound effects of the bullet exploded in my ears, made me see stars for a moment.

I know, I know, I know.

Thomas's tombstone, me in a cast, the rain.

The applause.

"I want to tell you something," Kai said, when we were cleaning up and getting ready to go to the after party. "Stop what you're doing for a minute."

I shut the lid of the costume bin and turned around to face him.

"So you know I won't be here next year, right?"

"Yeah."

"And you know that this isn't the end."

I stared at him. He got up from the chair he was sitting on and came to stand in front of me.

"I want you to be the new me," he said. "I want you to take over next year."

I felt like I'd been shot up with a lightning bolt. "What? *Me*, take over?"

"Yeah, of course."

"What's so great about me? I mean, why not choose someone else?"

Kai picked up a box on the desk and put it on the shelf above us. "Don't you know you're special?"

He turned back to me and patted my head. "Don't you know you've always been the most reliable, the most flexible? Like a sweet little brother. Always so willing."

So willing. A thousand different kinds of emotion rushed in like adrenaline. I started to say something, but he laughed softly and took his phone out of his jeans pocket.

"My girl's here," he said. "I gotta go. Call me, okay? This isn't the end."

He put on his jacket, squeezed my shoulder, and went out. I stood there staring through the door, not knowing what to think. So willing, he said.

Keira was waiting by the back doors, sitting on the steps with a bouquet of yellow roses.

"Hey, beautiful," she said, kissing me. "Take these. Let's go."

For once, there was no music playing in the car. I told her about an after party at Vanessa Jacoby's house and asked if she wanted to go.

"If you want to."

"I don't."

"Then what do you want to do?"

"Anything."

We drove around looking for a fancy restaurant and talking about the play until Keira pointed out the window and said, "We have to stop here."

I thought she'd found us a nice diner, but it turned out to be the town playground.

"What's here?" I asked.

I parked and she unbuckled her seatbelt. "I have to show you something. Come on."

I got out and followed her through the gate. The place was dark and deserted. I felt around for her hand and held onto it. She went behind the swing set and under the monkey bars and started climbing on top of the jungle gym, hissing for me to come up. I rolled my eyes about it but I went up.

I found her at the top, lying on her back with her head inside the tube slide.

"What are you doing?" I asked her.

"Shh. Lie down. Look up."

The static on the bottom shocked the back of my neck. "Where?"

"There," she said, using her phone as a flashlight, and then I saw it: tiny letters carved into the plastic. *When I grow up, the me from then will be better than the me from now.*

"When I was little, I got this Swiss Army knife from my uncle for my birthday. My dad said I should take care of it, use it when I went camping with the Girl Scouts and whatever. He figured I'd be special because none of the other girls would have one. I always hated that kind of thing…I'd wanted ice skates, not a knife."

I imagined Keira as a kid. A sad little girl in a brown skirt and yellow shirt covered in badges, sitting where our faces were now, carving words into the slide. "Why did you write that?"

She put her phone down, and I couldn't see the writing anymore. "I thought it was possible, back then."

We came out of the slide and stayed on the jungle gym. There was nothing to do, and we started trying to count the stars.

This is what it means, I thought. *Treasure what doesn't last forever.*

We were there together, taking it all in. The whole world was quiet, like the sky was listening to us and our agelessness.

MAY

We are in Dr. Scheinberg's office because my parents have discovered that I haven't been taking my medication.

"I caught him in the act," my dad says. "I caught him flushing them down the toilet."

Dr. Scheinberg is unfazed, just looks at me like I'm a piece of translucent film. "Jordan, do you understand that when you are sick, you need to take medication in order to get better?"

"Yeah," I tell her. "Yeah, of course."

"So if you know that this is very important, why don't you take yours?"

"Because I'm not sick."

"Jordan," my mom says. "Don't start with this."

"Start with *what*?"

Dr. Scheinberg turns to my parents and says, "He's in denial."

"Please, if you're going to talk about me, say it to *me*, not them."

"Jordan, I think you're in denial."

"As in denying what?"

"Your depression and post-traumatic stress disorder."

I resist the urge to say fuck. "I don't have depression or PTSD, that's the thing. I'm not going to take meds for problems I don't even have."

"But you do have problems," my dad says. "Dr. Scheinberg is here to help you. If you had been able to help yourself, we wouldn't have gotten her."

"Don't you want to feel better?" my mom asks me. "Don't you want to take the medication so you can feel better?"

"I don't want to rely on a bunch of pills to make me happy for the rest of my life."

"No one is making you rely on pills to be happy."

"But that's what it looks like! That's what it looks like you want me to do! It has nothing to do with getting better!"

"Calm down," Dr. Scheinberg says. "Lower your voice."

"Sure, sure. I bet now you're going to say I have anger issues and prescribe me some pills to take care of that. So I can live the rest of my life strung out on meds like some—"

"Like some what?"

She is actually looking at me. I glare back at her.

"Like who?" she asks, leaning forward.

"Nothing," I tell her. "Nobody."

"You think it's the same, don't you?" There is some empathy in her face. Sadness, maybe, or pity. "It's the same to you."

"Where are you going?" my mom asks me.

"Nowhere. The waiting room. You guys talk, I'll wait for you."

I open the door and sit near the receptionist's desk, counting the change in my pockets to see if I have enough for a two-dollar pack of Skittles. Five of my quarters spill out and roll underneath the chairs.

"Dammit," I say, getting down on my hands and knees.

I know it isn't the same. It's totally different.

But Keira needs things to feel better. That's her, not me.

MAY

You're going to move on.

You're going to get better.

I will help you, I promise.

She is speaking with her shoulder pressed against mine, her arm around me, apologizing for trying to kiss me when I didn't want it.

"Don't say sorry," I whisper. "It's my fault. It's my problem."

She says, "It's not your fault."

"It is, Elizabeth."

"I'm in love with you, Jordan."

We're lying on the grass looking up, holding hands, drinking soda from one can. I can hear the music from inside the hall where the Social is being held. Out here, we are so far away. The world is vast and the sky is endless.

"I know."

"So what do you think of me?"

I remember Keira and me, counting the stars. Elizabeth helping me with pre-calc, lending me her novels, coming over to teach me how to keep my room clean. Keira, someone I need to let go of; Elizabeth, present and real and here with me.

"I think you're beautiful."

And suddenly I'm transported back to December thirty-first of sophomore year, when I tried not to think about turning sixteen because I knew she wasn't going to be there, and how my mom and dad tried to make me happy by inviting my aunt and her family over, and how my cousins made fun of me for being lovesick. I can remember going outside to shovel the snow in the driveway at eleven-thirty in the night even though there was no point because it was still snowing, and all of a sudden there was a rush of wind and somebody crashed into me and it was Keira, and my breath was gone.

"Aren't you supposed to be in rehab?" I'd whispered, rubbing snowflakes out of my eyes to see her clearer.

She took my face into her hands and kissed my forehead. "Yeah, but I had to come for you."

And even though she'd snuck out, and even though she might have been high, she'd come for me. I mean, *she'd come for me.*

But she was always sad. Somewhere inside of her there was this deep void of sadness that took over all of that beauty…

I hear Elizabeth start to cry.

"Hey," I say.

She's sitting up with her arms around her knees, her chin tucked to her chest. "I love you, Jordan. I love you so much."

I want to say I love her too. I do love her. I want to love her.

"I can't do that right now."

"I know."

"I hate it. I hate myself for it. I don't know, it hurts in so many places, when someone says something and when I think about certain things. I can't, I can't do anything. I'm stuck. It's my fault, I'm sorry."

She hesitates. "Do you want to talk about it?"

Talk about it. Crisscross of blue and green veins under olive skin, she is shaking, I think it's just her having one of those nightmares but it is her eighteen-year old brain being struck into oblivion by something I can only see an outline of in the dark, I *saw* it.

"I don't know how much you heard about it. But I did see her."

She is ripping blades of grass and sprinkling the pieces on her skirt. "So who saw you?"

"Her...her mom and dad." Punching me in the face. Hitting me and screaming.

"No, I mean, who *saw* you?"

She's staring at me, and I realize that I'm not afraid of her bones, that they might be made of porcelain, or her skin, if it tears like rice paper. She is not fragile that way. Ordinary is not solid. Ordinary is fragile.

I bury my face in her neck. Baby powder and soap. I think of her skin, firm and soft, and her scent. Baby powder and soap. I'd expected tears, but my eyes are dry. My eyes are dry, thank God, for the first time. I sit up again.

"Are you okay?"

"Yes."

"How is your eye?" She touches the patch so lightly that I don't even think to flinch. "Does it hurt?"

"Yes, but…" I take a deep breath. "I'm sorry."

"Don't say sorry." Elizabeth takes both of my hands and brings them to her heart. "I think you've gotten better. A little bit."

"Because of you."

"No, because that's what happens in life, you break and you rebuild and you come back. That's just what happens. Isn't it such a miracle?"

Isn't it such a miracle, she says, and I feel the tears come to my eyes now and I say, "The doctor said I can't cry," so instead she hugs me hard, hard enough to almost close the void of sadness passed onto me, just for a few minutes until she lets me go and asks me to let her cry for a little while. Not out of sorrow, but because she's happy—she is so happy. I don't get it.

She says, "The world is so beautiful tonight with you," and I say yeah, because my cheek is on her shoulder, and there is the baby powder and soap and her inhales and exhales that I want to drink in and swallow and become apart of. On our way back to the building after we find her shoes, she touches my hand and I think I feel alive again.

Entry# 17: Trying

There was once a boy who didn't want to wake up. He wasn't me. He stayed in bed with the covers over his head and closed his eyes and forgot about school and his parents and everyone who loved him. He tried, I mean. But you can't forget the way morning grass in the springtime feels on your hands as you reach to pick up a lacrosse ball, or the taste of fish turned over in the fire burning nearby, or the first time you ever kissed someone who made you feel like the world had stopped spinning. He remembered being spat on and running in the road and getting lost. When he called out to the people, no one bothered to stop. Nobody stops anymore.

It's okay because sometimes four walls became the cornfields he played in as a child before he learned that trespassing is an actual thing and bullying is both a noun and an adjective, before whipped cream and marshmallows stopped tasting good and words were no longer like the American continent to Christopher Columbus, and to him, which made them both a pair of really sick bastards. I guess. They thought he was sick but he honestly wasn't. He could've gotten up. He thought about it. He didn't do it.

"Close the curtains," he said, and forgot what the sun looked like, what colors he used to draw it with on paper, even the name and how to spell it, S-U-N. He was okay with that. People like this exist and they are fine.

I went to the cemetery with Elizabeth on Friday after school, bearing flowers and a CD I made, of songs I have a hard time listening to now. We took two buses and walked a long, long way (no car, we decided, because going through the struggle seemed much more decent) to the place, but when we finally got to the front I couldn't go in. I stood over the gate and looked out at all the tombstones.

"Look at how many people have died," was what I told Elizabeth, and she touched my shoulder and asked me if I was okay. I think the sun was in my eyes and I took off my glasses to rub them with my hand and said yeah. She said, "We can come back another time if you want."

"No. I can do it."

There are people who never get up and forget how to open the door and turn on the lights. They exist and are fine.

I put the CD on the dirt and the flowers next to the tombstone and read the inscription. Elizabeth squeezed my hand. "Ready to go?"

I wiped my hands on my jeans. Said yeah.

"Yeah," I told her. "I'm ready.

17313383R00138

Made in the USA
Middletown, DE
17 January 2015